The Realm of Senary

Hymn of Asperity and Avarice

D.L. William

The Realm of Senary: Hymn of Asperity and Avarice

The Library of Congress Cataloging-in-Publication Data is available upon request.

ISBN 978-0-578-80576-4 (Paperback)

First Edition: November 2020.

III

IV

Contents:

VI

Prologue

A tall man dressed in exquisite gold-plated armor, with intricate engravings on each heavy piece of steel stood motionless in a dark room. The moon illuminated only a sliver of the rooms innards through the cracked doorway. The room's silence is disturbed by troubled, sporadic breathing with the distinct hint of fear with each breath. The open window blows a warm summer air through the doorway, creaking the giant oak door open ever so softly. The armored man's stature is fully illuminated. His shoulders are broad, and his medium length hair is a shimmering silver draped over his face. Sweat is dripping down his short silver beard and falling onto the floor. The sweat is instantly mixed with the warm bright red liquid pooling on the hardwood floor. The pool is surrounding another man who lays lifeless on the floor. With each passing second more blood pools around him. The silver sword laying at the armored man's feet is coated finely in the same scarlet color, the same color that is dripping from his tense fingers. The overwhelming scent of death is filling the room and escaping into the hallway. A barrage of stomping and ear wrenching metal clanging is roaring down the hallway. Louder and louder it grows with each second, while at the same time it is as if the entire world has fallen silent and succumbed to the darkness of the human mind. The barrage suddenly stops, shadows cover everything in the room. A long pause disturbs the air, thirteen peering pairs of eyes are staring in shock at two men. One alive, and the other nothing more than a soulless corpse searching for a place to rest. In a single swift moment, an enormous man loses his grip on his emotions. Letting out a pain filled yell, his tears fall onto the blood pooled ground. He clenches his fist and strikes the armored man in the face as hard as he can. He falls to the ground and begins to choke seemingly on his own breath. The enormous man is towering over him, with the distinct feeling of intent to kill overwhelming the atmosphere. A woman dressed in a beautiful sequin dress falls to her knees next to the man's corpse. Her dress becomes saturated with the warm scarlet liquid that has pooled on the ground and tears fall like a river off her cheeks. The armored man begins gasping for air as he tries to speak, his face is turning purple, and his gasps are growing louder as everyone watches in disbelief and shock. The room fades to black as the clouds pass over the moon, the crying and mourning are broken by a loud thud as the armored man's head hits the blood-soaked floor as he falls unconscious.

The Realm of Senary
Hymn of Asperity and Avarice

X

Chapter 1: The Armor-Clad Loner

An arctic winter air blew through the mountains high above the town of Drixyl, the snow blew across the rocks like clouds kissing the ground. A party of three young adventurers are traversing the chilling landscape in search for their prey. They are two young women, and a younger boy. The women are in their early twenties, one elven, the other human. The young boy is a Lynx, the uncommon race among the demi-humans. Lynx are known for their cunning nature and agility. They are covered in a soft fur from head to toe, their snout and head the shape of a tiger. Each one with different markings through their fur.

The young human woman wraps her arms across her chest. "How much longer until we find it?"

"I don't know, quit your whining." The elven woman says in an annoyed tone walking forward through the deep snow of the mountains, trying to ignore the brisk winter air.

The human girl is angered by her tone, and scowls at her slightly as the snow pelts them in the bone chilling wind. The young women begin to shiver, their fingers are changing color and they are losing feeling. The small Lynx happily walking behind them is comfortable, he is dressed appropriately and has fur keeps him warm.

The Lynx points eastward in the direction of the harsh winds. "I think I see something over there."

He takes point and traverses through the slippery landscape, keeping his balance perfectly. The two women follow closely behind, the elf does not have much trouble traversing the mountain either, elves are quick on their feet. Most elves feel they are the superior race amongst the demi-humans but repress their thoughts out of kindness usually. The human girl on the other hand, is rather clumsy, often tripping and slipping. She carefully walks, moving slowly eastward. She begins to fall behind and soon loses sight of the two other members of her party. She calls out to them, but the winds howling carries her fearful voice astray. A shiver shakes down her spine, a combination of

nervousness and impending hypothermia.

Suddenly she hears a blood curdling scream from in

front of her. That of a young boy.

"Isaiah!" She screams but no answer returns.

Suddenly the young woman is knocked off

her feet, as if a rock hit her in the chest. She falls

backwards and hits her head off the rocky ground.

She examines the object in her hands as she opens

her eyes. She lifts the object and feels a soft fur. Her

eyes widen with horror, as she is holding the

severed head of her fellow adventurer Isaiah, the

Lynx. Blood drips from the Lynx's severed head

covering her torso and legs with blood. She screams

and drops the head; she crawls away backwards in

horror with her eyes locked on the head as if they

were glued there for eternity. Another scream rings through her ears, a woman's. The young woman looks up into the white abyss in front of her, when a severed leg covered in fur and a leather pant leg with a shredded armor plate slams the ground next to her.

The young woman lets out a piercing squeal of horror. "That armor... it's Estelle's!" She cries out.

The air is freezing her tears as they fall down her face, and all she can see is steam coming from the severed leg from the blood that is pouring on the ground melting the snow. She cries and screams her friends' names at the top of her lungs. From the white abyss appears a tall figure, nearly eight feet in height and covered in icy fur. It's eyes glowing red like a fire, striking fear in the young woman's mind.

She screams and tries to crawl away as fast as she

can, but the beast stomps after her. The beast grabs

her leg and lifts her up like a twig, hanging upside

down with her face inches from the monsters and

shrieks at the woman hanging. The shriek chills her

bones worse than the arctic temperatures of the

mountain, she cries for help and tries to break free

from the monster's grip but cannot escape. The

beast takes her arm and examines her like a child

playing with its food, it slowly pulls her leg and

arm. She screams in pain, crying for help. Just

before the beast rips her in half, a blade is thrusted

through the beast's chest. The shock makes the beast

drop the woman; she crawls away in tears trying to

understand how she managed to escape. The beast

screams in pain, as the sword is pulled swiftly from

its torso. The monster flails and swings violently in

every direction to fend off the attacker, before the

beast can find the swordsman the same blade is run

through its neck. The beast coughs blood and falls

to its knees gasping for air. The swordsman appears

from the white abyss, adorned in bloody steel gray

plate armor, and a white cloak over his shoulders

draping down his back. His helmet has only a few

openings, it's a great helm with two openings for

his eyes, and a few holes for his mouth. There are

two curved horns reaching skyward. His chest plate

and cloak have a black rune aligned in the middle.

The beast glares at the warrior with its menacing

red eyes just before a blade slices deep into its

muscular neck. Its head falls to the ground with a

frightened expression. Blood gushes from the beast's neck and its body falls to the ground. The armored warrior wiped the blood on his black moleskin gloves and sheaths his sword and collects the beast's head. He traverses the landscape to find the elven woman who'd almost been killed by the beast. He approaches her as she is unconscious and bleeding from her arm. He takes his cloak off and wraps it around her as he lifts her into his arms.

"Let's go." He says in a deep calm tone to the young human girl shaking in fear.

She manages to stand and follows the man who saved their lives, shocked over the loss of her friend. Soon they arrive at a campsite in a small cave. The man places the cloak wrapped elf down gently next to a pile of logs and rocks and lights a small fire to warm the two up.

"Sir, is she going to be alright?" The blonde human girl asks with a shiver in her voice.

"Yeah, the yetari had a hold of her for a moment while she was trying to save the lynx. She cut her pant leg and slipped free. Before I was able to strike it swung and knocked her unconscious. I already healed her wounds with the little bit of magic I know, but she'll need to rest. I'm sorry I couldn't help your friend." He says softly in a deep tone, placing more wood atop the fire.

She begins to cry and weep for her friend. The man throws her another cloak from his satchel. It's not as thick as the one he wrapped the elven woman in, but it's warm enough to help fight the freezing cold temperature.

The man stands and walks towards the mouth of the cave. "Stay here until I return."

"Where are you going?" The woman asks with a quiver in her voice.

"There's likely more than one. It's rare to see a yetari alone in the mountains."

"Wait it's dangerous!" She yells out but he vanishes into the thick white snow being blown violently across the mountain tops. "He doesn't even have a cloak..." she says to herself as she looks over towards her elven partner.

Soon the elf opens her eyes, they're a vibrant amethyst and glowing from the sparkle of the bright white wind. She sits up quickly in a panic, her lavender colored hair falls over her face as she whips her head back and forth.

"Yovanna, where is Isaiah?!" She asks with desperation in her voice as she looks at the blonde human woman. Yovanna comforts her with a hug as tears flow down her cheeks.

"He didn't make it, Estelle." She sobs.

Tears slowly leak from Estelle's eyes. "What happened!?"

"That monster…killed him, but an armored swordsman saved us. Or else we'd both be dead."

Estelle feels Yovanna's arms for wounds. "Yovanna, are you alright? Are you injured?

Yovanna takes Estelle's hands and pushes her backwards, surveying her arms and legs for any gashes. "Yes, I'm fine. That man said that he healed your wounds too. You were cut open."

"Where is he?" Estelle asks curiously.

Yovanna looks to the mouth of the cave as a harsh wind blows inward. "He left. He said there were more out there."

"What do you mean he left!? What a jackass!? Where's his party?" Estelle flails her arms in anger.

"He didn't have one. He was alone." Yovanna says with a soft tone, thinking of their savior.

"Alone...?" Estelle sits back and holds her knees to her chest.

"Yes. But he slayed the monster, he said it was a yetari... perhaps his party met a similar fate?"

"Have you seen him before?" Estelle asks curiously

"I have around town once or twice." Yovanna says as she points to Estelle's thick fur lined white cloak. "That's his cloak you're wearing."

Estelle looks down and feels the cloak, examining the marking on the back.

"A rune?"

"I don't know, he just appeared and brought us back here. He carried you back and started a fire for us, then just left again." Yovanna raises her shoulders in confusion.

Their conversation is interrupted with a shriek that echoes through the mountain tops. The two women look to the mouth of the cave and see a splatter of blood coat the white ground.

"Graaaah!" A painful yell rings through their ears from outside of the cave.

Yovanna trembles in fear as she closely watches the mouth of the cave. Estelle is watching curiously, clutching her swords hilt tight, ready to strike.

A loud thud shakes the ground, and the sound of flesh being split rings through their ears, sending a shiver down their spine. More blood flows into the already coated snow, and another thud shakes the cave again, but this one was far more violent than the last. The wind picks up and the blood fades into the freezing white air.

Both women are sitting completely still, both closely watching the entrance to the cave. Only the flickering of the fire is making a peep. A tall figure approaches the mouth of the cave. Yovanna begins to shake in fear again, but Estelle is still ready to strike at any moment.

"Move over! Quickly!" A deep stern voice says from the mouth of the cave.

Yovanna quickly slides towards Estelle, and the armor-clad warrior falls on his back near where Yovanna was sitting next to the fire.

The man rips a piece of cloth from his tunic underneath his armor. "Ah, God damn yetari's. They're the only God damn creature that goes for the thighs first. What type of creature does that!?"

"You're bleeding!" Yovanna says in shock.

Estelle is in shock over the armored man who is soaked in blood.

"I'll be fine. Just gotta patch this wound before I lose too much blood." He says.

"Let me do that for you. Can you use your magic to close the wound?" Yovanna takes the torn cloth from his hand and begins to wrap his wound.

"Not at the moment, If I use too much of my stamina to heal myself, I might lose consciousness from the overexertion." He groans in pain as the cloth touches his open wound.

"Hey, jackass." Estelle says with a frustrated tone.

"Pardon me?" He asks.

"Who in their right mind fights monsters alone? Especially up here?"

"Estelle, stop it. He saved us." Yovanna says trying to calm down her enraged friend, who's seemingly forgotten her fallen party member already.

The man looks at her for a moment but turns away and ignores her.

"Hey! Don't ignore me! You're not even dressed for this weather! You're an idiot!" She exclaims as she grows more and more frustrated.

"You're one to talk. You're an elf, you're up here in breezy summer attire, no means of warmth. Besides, I was dressed appropriately. But you needed that cloak more than I." He says with a deep voice.

Estelle remains quiet and calms down, noticing that he gave her his means of cold weather survival. He stares at Estelle for a moment, examining her thoroughly. Estelle is staring back at him for a moment before turning away with embarrassment.

"He has steel blue eyes, they're beautiful, and youthful." Estelle thinks to herself amidst her embarrassment. A smile peeks through her aggression.

The armor-clad man continues to stare at Estelle, seemingly struck by some mysterious force putting him in a daze. He shakes his head and looks away.

"There. All done." Yovanna says with a sweet smile.

"Okay, it's time to get off this mountain. The storm is only going to get worse." He says, bracing himself on the side of the rocky cave as he stands.

"Shouldn't we wait until morning?" Yovanna asks.

"No. A storm like this could easily cause the cave to be swallowed by the snow. Let's go." He says.

"Wait a second, tell me your name." Estelle demands.

"It's best neither of you know." He pauses for a moment before gathering the heads of the slain beasts.

"Okay fine then, Mr. mysterious. Why were you staring at me then?" Estelle demands.

"You... I apologize."

The armored man gathers his items in the cave, as he steps out onto the cold mountain top, he looks around and is nearly knocked off his feet from a strong gust of wind billowing down from the peak of the mountains.

He turns his head to the two women in the cave. "This is getting worse by the second. We've got to hurry."

Yovanna is the first to stand, she's shaking still, not from the cold but from the shock and anxiety of the events that had just transpired. Estelle uses the cave walls to steady herself as she tries to stand. As she stands, she nearly falls back over and holds her head.

Yovanna holds Estelle's arm as she tries to steady herself. "Estelle are you okay?"

"Yes, I'm fine, I was just dizzy for a moment." Estelle says as she looks towards the mouth of the cave. The tall broad man is staring over his shoulder at her, carefully watching her every move.

Yovanna helps Estelle towards the mouth of the cave.   Let's not wait."

The two young women follow the stoic armored man down the mountain. He's keeping a steady pace with a wide gate, but he is noticing the two accompanying him are falling behind. He slows his pace for them to keep up, but the storm is becoming more violent with each step they take.

"This is why I work alone; I don't have to worry about the safety of anyone else." He says to himself under his breath, shaking his head slowly.

He looks down and notices that he's bleeding through his bandages already, he lets out a sigh and continues at the slow but steady pace, periodically checking on the two women following him behind closely. Their pace is slowing more and more. The wind and heavy snowfall are making their descent more and more difficult, and a strong wind knocks over Estelle and Yovanna.

"Estelle! Wake up! Estelle!" Yovanna shouts trying to wake her unconscious friend.

"She lost too much blood to handle this descent down. Can you still walk?" He asks sternly as he rewraps Estelle in the cloak, he had given her.

"I can, but I'm not leaving without Estelle!" Yovanna yells out.

He looks Yovanna in the eyes with a sincere glare. "I know that, keep your voice down. Last thing we need is an avalanche because you want to start yelling at me."

Yovanna's face turns from an angry stare to a concerned look of terror as she covers her mouth as a child would. The armored man unstraps his chest piece and hands it to Yovanna, his back now only covered by the wool tunic that was under his armor. Yovanna examines the piece of armor, almost too heavy for her to carry, it's solid steel and lined with some sort of fabric, nothing like she's seen before. The armor clad man drops the severed heads of the yetari's and lifts Estelle onto his back holding her tightly so that she does not slip off, the wind instantly turns the armored swordsman's pale exposed neck from a white that's brighter than the snow that's falling, to a bright red as if it were burned by a flame.

"Come here and make sure she's fully covered and put on that chest piece. I don't want to lose it." He says sternly to Yovanna. She obeys and straps on the chest piece that's giant in comparison to her body, then covers Estelle's unconscious face with the hood of the armor-clad man's cloak.

Yovanna finishes wrapping Estelle with the cloak. "Okay, she's covered."

"Let's get moving." He says in a deep voice as they pick up their pace and trot down the mountain side.

The grizzly wind and heavy snowfall quickly weather the trio, the man's step is becoming more sporadic as he loses more and more blood. Yovanna watches the man closely as they continue down the mountain, she notices that everywhere his clothing is ripped has turned to a similar red as his neck besides one spot on his left arm, it's as black as night but it's a design of some sort.

"Sir, are you going to be okay without your armor, it's very warm and I can tell you're getting colder." She asks while covering her eyes from a rough patch of wind.

"I'll be fine. Can you keep up if I pick up my pace?" He looks back and says loudly.

"Yes, I'll do my best." Yovanna nods in agreeance.

"Don't fall behind." He changes his pace from a fast-careful walk to a large gated trot. His eyes wince in pain with each step he takes on his wounded leg. He's carefully holding Estelle slightly above his body so that she doesn't get shaken up too much by his walk. Yovanna struggles to keep up with the man carrying her friend but manages until they reach the base of the mountain.

The man stops for a moment and lays Estelle up against a tree, he examines her closely, checking for frostbite and making sure she is still breathing steadily.

"Is she going to be okay?" Yovanna asks, holding the chest piece close to her body with her arms.

"She'll be fine, we'd better get her to a doctor to be sure." He says as he takes her in his arms this time and holds her closely as he begins to walk again.

His pained walk has turned into a limp, and the warm air escaping from his helmet is becoming more unsteady, but he holds strong, keeping Estelle held closely to his body. Yovanna walks beside him carefully, watching him closely. She notices his leg is bleeding, leaving a trail of red directly behind them with each step.

Yovanna stops in her tracks; her eyes widen quickly. "Sir, are you okay!? You're bleeding from your wound profusely!"

"I'm fine. Worry about your friend." He says sternly as he refuses to break his stride.

Yovanna scowls with a certain hint of anger and concern for the man carrying her friend, she sighs softly and continues next to him. The snow that bombarded their journey down the mountain comes to a silent halt as the sun fades over the mountain.

Yovanna opens the door to the doctor's building, holding it as the armored man carries her friend inside. He ignores the attendant at the front desk and carries her upstairs without a single iota of care for anyone else.

"Excuse me! Please check in first!" The attendant yells as she watches as the armored man carries what seems to be a lifeless body up the stairs.

Yovanna stops the attendant from halting the man's pace. "I'm sorry. Her name is Estelle Fellistar, could a doctor please see her. She was injured and lost consciousness on a quest."

"Oh, yes. I'll have a doctor see her right away. Is there anyone else that requires attention?" She asks, writing notes on a piece of paper quickly.

Yovanna grimaces towards the stairs. "The man carrying her is injured as well, but I'm not quite sure that he'll be willing to speak to a doctor."

The woman looks over her glasses at Yovanna. "Okay, what's his name?"

"He wouldn't tell us, is Estelle going to be alright?"

"Oh, I'll ask him then. Our doctors are the best in Senary. Your friend will be just fine, I'm sure." The attendant says as she gestures Yovanna to follow her upstairs. The two quickly walk upstairs but as they reach the top, they are stopped by the armored man abruptly.

"She's in that first room. Can I have my armor back?" He asks.

"Oh, yes." Yovanna says as she lifts the heavy plate armor from her body and hands it back to the man who hastily straps it back on himself and limps downstairs as blood continues to trail behind him.

"Hey! Where are you going!? You need to see a doctor!" Yovanna yells out to the man who is ignoring her. He exits the building and closes the door quickly behind him.

"What's with that man?" The attendant asks.

Yovanna shakes her head. "I have no idea, he's very kind but he's like a brick wall when you try to speak with him."

"Is he from around here? I've never seen him before." The attendant asks with a newly sparked curiosity.

"I don't know..." Yovanna begins to say but is startled by an intense bang on the outside of the building. She runs downstairs with the attendant and hurries outside. As they emerge and look around, the armored man is laying on his side on the ground just to the right of the door.

"Oh dear, I'll get someone to help carry him in!" The attendant says in a panic. She quickly returns with two men in doctors' garbs who struggle to lift the man from the ground. Yovanna watches silently, still in shock over the events of the day. The men carry him inside and up the stairs carefully while Yovanna and the attendant follow them.

"You can wait downstairs or in the room with Estelle. We'll get him taken care of." The attendant says to Yovanna who is staring intently up the stairs, seemingly afraid to take another step. She bites her cheek and slowly steps upstairs and into Estelle's room.

"Oh Estelle, please be okay." She says softly to Estelle while she sits on the foot of her bed.

Night is quick to pass, and the sun is hasty as it rises. The sun kisses the ground outside illuminating the soft snowfall hugging the already white and glistening world. The streets outside are quickly filled with merchants and warriors alike, each one blissfully enjoying their early morning conversing and treading through the already deep snow on the streets.

Estelle is the first to wake in her bed. She rises and sits on the edge to stretch, letting out a big yawn and smiling as if she were uninjured at all. She looks around the sunlit room to see Yovanna sleeping in a chair just at the foot of the bed, softly and silently asleep in the uncomfortable wooden chair. She looks around some more then examines herself, noticing she is only wearing her pants and light blue shirt.

"What happened to my armor?" Estelle asks herself quietly. "Yovanna wake up. Where are we?" Yovanna wakes and stretches, cracking her stiff body from the uncomfortable sleeping position she was in.

"You're up early." She says with a yawn and another big stretch. "We're at the doctors, you passed out when we were coming down the mountain."

"I did what? How did we end up here?" Estelle raises her eyebrows in confusion.

"The armored guy carried you the rest of the way." Yovanna smiles.

"He carried me all the way down the mountain?" Estelle is struck by Yovanna's statement.

"Yes, I'm surprised you don't remember. I could have sworn you were awake for a little bit of the trip."

"I don't remember much after leaving the cave."

Yovanna smiles happily towards her friend. "The doctors said you lost a little too much blood, but you were going to make a full recovery."

"What happened to him?" Estelle asks.

"He left after bringing you here, then he passed out outside. He's in the next room. He was injured himself; he was bleeding most of the way down the mountain, but he wouldn't stop. He just said to worry about you and not him."

"Honestly, what a thick-headed idiot that guy is. Let's go wake him up." Estelle says as she stands and stretches once more, fully healed and ready for the day ahead.

The two walk out of the room and look around the hall, not a soul in sight. They quietly tiptoe to the next room over and open the creaking oak door slowly peeking in.

"There's no one in here." Estelle says softly to Yovanna.

Yovanna raises her shoulders in confusion. "He was there last night, maybe they moved him."

The two amid their confusion are interrupted by the attendant from yesterday.

"Good morning you two. Are you feeling well, Ms. Fellistar?" She asks sweetly.

"I'm feeling great, thanks. Where's the armored guy at?" Estelle asks without hesitation.

"Oh, he checked out last night. He woke up shortly after the doctors healed him and refused any more treatment."

"He what!?" Estelle exclaims, flush red with anger.

"Yes… he left. But he paid your bill in full."

"Oh my… I'm really starting to hate that guy." Estelle says as she shakes her head in her hand. "Did he by chance tell you his name or did you at least see his face?"

The attendant blushes a little with a smile. "He refused to tell us his name, but I did see his face."

Estelle grabs the attendant by the shoulders and shakes her with caring intensity. "What did he look like!?"

"Calm down!" She says as she frees herself. "He was young, around my age, early twenties, with a short silver beard, and long silver hair. He had rather pretty eyes now that I think about it, light blue, very handsome." She says as she begins to romanticize her interaction with him in her head.

"Did anyone else see him?" Yovanna asks.

"No, only me. I took off his helmet just before he woke up. The doctors don't pay mind to armor since they heal with magic. I was just curious for paperwork…" She says with a hint of embarrassment.

"Okay, thanks for the help." Estelle says as the curiosity grows deeper for the armored man who helped her and her friends. She runs back into her room and gathers her things, readying herself for the day but notices the soft white cloak laying on the bed where she was. She picks it up and smells it quietly, before wrapping herself in it again.

Yovanna turns her head, trying to look away from the outlandish act. "Estelle, why are you smelling that?"

Estelle smiles putting on the cloak. "To get his scent, this is his cloak, right? If I smell him in town, I'll be able to point him out better. I'm an elf, we have spectacular senses."

"If you say so." Yovanna mumbles as she shakes her head and exits the room soon followed by Estelle. They open the door to the busy early morning streets to be bombarded with the sunlight and dozens of townsfolk talking and gallivanting in the streets.

Yovanna lets out a yawn. "I'm going home, I need more sleep in my own bed. What are you going to do?"

"I'm going to try and find that man. I know what he looks like now, so hopefully I can find out where he is." She says with determination in her voice.

"Have fun with that. I'm staying in tonight, so I'll see you tomorrow." Yovanna waves and disappears into the busy streets.

Estelle thinks to herself for a moment, pondering over the possible places she'll see her armored idiot. "I've got it, I'll just wait in the guild hall!" She exclaims happily in the middle of the streets. People all around look at her for a moment, then ignore her as if she didn't exist.

Traversing the busy streets is an easy task for the nimble elf, quickly she finds her destination which is even busier than the streets outside. She can barely open the door, dozens of warriors and mages alike are all huddled together in the guild hall excited to pick their days work. She pushes through the thick crowd of people all huddled in the center and reaches the main desk in the back of the building.

"Excuse me, has an armored guy been here, two horns, quiet, annoying, and probably alone?" She asks the woman sitting at the desk.

"Well, let's see." She says as she looks around the crowded building. "There's some horns, there's some horns, there's some more." The guild attendant says with a hint of arrogance.

Estelle scowls at the woman behind the desk. "Okay, I can see how you're feeling today. He's tall, he'd be towering above most of these people in here. He's wearing all silver armor, and he's usually wearing this cloak."

"Excuse me miss. I believe I know of a man that fits your description. Come with me to my office." An older gentleman says calmly to Estelle peeking out from the door next to the bookshelf in the back.

"Thank you." Estelle says with a smile to the old man, as she passed the woman at the desk, she glances over with a smug scowl and throws her nose in the air as she confidently walks into the room.

"Have a seat miss." He says as he closes the door and takes his seat behind the desk. "So, this armored, annoying, quiet, loner you're looking for. What business do you have with him?"

Estelle smiles happily. "He helped us while we were on the mountain hunting the monster, and I was injured. He carried me down the mountain and took me to the doctors, along with paying my bill. I'd like to ask him a few questions and probably smack him in the face."

The old gentleman turns his head in curiosity. "Why would you wish to harm him, after he helped you even though you are a stranger to him?"

Estelle's smile deteriorates into an annoyed scowl. "Because, he deserves it. He didn't even tell me his name."

"That's not an adequate answer." He says as he leans on the desk.

"Fine." She says with an annoyed sigh. "We lost a member of our party yesterday to what he called a yetari, I want to know why he couldn't kill the beast sooner, so we didn't lose him."

The man shakes his head over Estelle's arrogance. "So, you're another failed adventurer wondering why there wasn't a knight in shining armor to save everyone in the world."

"No!"

"Listen close. These contracts all merit the need for someone willing to do the job of the unable. That's where the guild comes into play, we merely judge the skill level necessary required to complete the contracts. I remember the mountain beast contract, I posted it nearly a month ago. In big bold lettering, I said that this requires someone able to fight that equal to a King's army to complete. Yet, you decided it would be adequate to take the quest. Correct?" The man retorts with sheer arrogance and anger.

"Yes…"

He leans back in his chair crossing his arms. "And this was the fallout. People die in this world, it's the harsh truth of it all. If you are unable to accept that fact, I advise changing your career path."

Estelle lowers her head into her hands and tears begin to fall softly into her lap. "I can handle it! I understand people will die… I do. It's just, why couldn't it have been me?"

"I believe in very few things, one being the capable, two being the value of monetary gain in this world, and that the Gods roll the dice of fate. If you lived, and your party member died. It means two things. They were not capable, and you were. The Gods rolled the dice in your favor that day. Do what you will with that information."

Estelle falls silent for a moment, pondering over the words just spoken to her.

"Is there anything else, any other reason you're looking for this man?" He asks, now growing annoyed by her childish reasoning.

"I need to know why he carried me down the mountain, why he didn't try to save himself when he was more injured than I, why he paid my hospital bill, and why he just disappeared out of nowhere." Estelle says as she dries her eyes and returns her scowl.

"I haven't known him for very long, so I can't give just reason behind his actions. Although he's very kind, he lives for his own reasons. I have not deciphered the man's internal workings, although I know that he is somewhat of a specter. He appears early in the morning before anyone else is awake and returns late in the evening after everyone has fallen into their dreams."

Estelle leans forward towards the desk. "Do you know his name?"

"That is something I wish not to divulge to anyone. He respects his privacy, and I respect that." He says.

"Do you mind if I wait here until the evening, it's my best chance at seeing him again."

"Do as you wish. I advise you to wait in here; it will be rather rowdy until nightfall. Feel free to use my bookshelf to pass the time." He says with a kind smile.

"Thank you." She says as she looks to the large bookshelf in the corner of the room.

"By the way, miss. I haven't introduced myself. My name is Johnathan Ryker, I am the master of this guild. What is your name?"

"My name is Estelle Fellistar. Pleasure to meet you, Mr. Ryker."

"Fellistar? As in the providence in the south?"

"Yes, my mother's side is the founding family of the land."

"Interesting. Perhaps we have more to talk of in due time." Johnathan stands and exits his office. Estelle pays no attention to his words and takes a large book from the bookshelf.

"Monsters of Senary." She reads to herself quietly before sitting in a comfortable chair in the corner and opening the large book. She dives into the book and glues herself to the seat. The day passes swiftly as Estelle reads every page in detail in the book, taking notes in her notebook of the characteristics of every monster.

Nightfall comes with much haste, and the people of Drixyl are all turning in for the evening. The guild empties out along with the street, only a few are roaming around still enjoying the chilly night air, gazing at the stars above through the breaks in the clouds. The only lights in sight are the torches fastened to the town's gates, and the dim lights behind the glass windows along the street sides. A cold wind flutters the powdered top of the snow across the fields creating a beautiful feeling of winter throughout the world.

"Your knight in shining armor should be returning soon, I advise you wait in the hall for him. Oh, you've almost finished that entire book…" Johnathan says curiously to Estelle while peeking through the door.

"Yes, I've found it so interesting." She says as she closes the book and returns it to the shelf.

"Go ahead and keep it. I have another copy in my personal study."

"Are you sure?"

"Yes, positive. Most people give no attention to the details of their career path. That book was what helped me when I was in your shoes. It'll help you as well."

Estelle smiles cheerfully. "Thank you, very much Mr. Ryker."

"Please, call me Johnathan. Mr. Ryker makes me sound… old." He chuckles and walks away. Estelle smiles and packs the book carefully in her satchel and enters the guild hall to find a seat.

"It's quiet, and empty." She says as she looks around, examining everything in the guild hall. "There're monster heads from all over the region hung on the wall, they seem fresh though." She says softly to herself.

"They are. I didn't start having them preserved until a certain someone started bringing them back." Johnathan chuckles.

"Bringing them back?" Estelle looks towards the preserved heads in curiosity.

Johnathan shakes his head with a smile. "Yes, your man in question is quite… adamant on bringing the heads of the slain beasts as proof of contract completion."

"I see…" Estelle says to herself as she continues to examine all the heads hung upon the walls.

"This place is beautiful, how long ago was it built?" She looks around slowly.

"Oh, not long ago. Maybe forty years? I built it with my father when I saved enough money from my days as a hunter. My father was an architect and was a perfectionist, every piece of wood was hand carved by us. If he didn't like it. He would throw it away and start over."

"Wow." Estelle says as she gazes around at the perfectly symmetrical patterns carved into the wooden walls and trim.

In the middle of her examination, a large oak door opening slowly shatters her focus.

"That's probably him." Johnathan says as he nudges Estelle and returns to his office. Estelle blushes slightly, nervous of seeing him again.

A tall man covered in frozen silver armor with two horns piercing the sky walks through the door. Carrying three frozen yetari heads roped together in one hand, and the other moleskin gloved hand gripping the hair of another bleeding severed head of a larger Yeti. Ignoring the presence of Estelle in the silent building, he walks through the building dripping blood and snow on the ground towards Johnathan's office.

"Hey!" Estelle yells to him but he ignores her call entering the office and closing the door. She runs to the door with excitement but can only hear muffled voices behind the closed door, soon followed by counting of coins on a desk. She sniffs the air, smelling the wafting scent, the same as the cloak's aroma.

"She's waiting outside." She hears behind the door. She quickly backs away and stands with her hands together staring intently at the door. It soon swings open and her eyes meet a pair of light blue eyes behind a frozen silver helmet being illuminated by a covered torch just outside of the office.

"Glad to see you're alright." He says with a surprising cheerful tone.

"I've waited all day! What the hell is wrong with you!? It's not polite to make someone wait!"

"Wonderful, I'll be leaving now." He says in a stern deep voice and walks past her.

Estelle stomps her foot in anger. "Wait! We're not done."

"Yes, we are."

Estelle runs and stands in front of him with her arms out, impeding his path to the board of contracts. "Why? Why are you... why are you the way that you are!?" Estelle says with a scowl and hint of resentment in her voice.

The man looks down at Estelle. "I don't understand your question."

"Why would you carry me down the mountain when you were badly injured!? Why would you pay my doctors bill, then just... just leave!?" She yells. He sighs and reaches around her taking a paper from the board and reads it silently. "Give me that! We're having a conversation!" Estelle yells again trying to swipe the paper from his hand, but he raises his arm and reads it above his head where she cannot reach.

"It's not a conversation if I don't partake."

Estelle crosses her arms in frustration. "You're absolutely insufferable, do you know that?"

"I try my best." He says still reading, making Estelle grit her teeth with anger. Johnathan watches from his office, chuckling quietly over their interaction.

Johnathan closes the door to his office as his chuckles fade away. "You two play nice now."

"Take off your helmet." Estelle demands.

"Why?" The man asks, looking towards the paper above his head.

Estelle looks up with just her eyes. "Because I'm going to slap you."

"That would defeat the purpose of wearing a helmet."

She shakes her head. "I hate you."

"You're not the first." He says as he folds the paper in his hand and places it into a bag fastened to his hip. "Johnathan, I'll be gone for a while. I'm taking this contract near Levenwood." He says loud enough for Johnathan to hear.

"Alright, stay safe." He says from behind his door.

"I'm going with you." Estelle says, crossing her arms and staring at the armored man towering above her.

He walks past her towards the door. "I'm going alone. Last time you were on a contract you almost lost your life. Find a new career."

Estelle throws her arms to the side to defend her self-respect. "I would have been fine! It just snuck up on me!"

The man stops and turns to Estelle. "A twelve feet tall yetari doesn't have the ability to sneak. They're far too clumsy and their bodies are too cumbersome. They have no natural predators; therefore, they haven't adapted the ability to sneak."

"Okay mister smart guy. Then teach me about these monsters." Estelle says, still staring intently at him.

He looks at her slightly confused and caught off guard by her demand. "I don't take students."

Estelle smiles. "Don't see me as a student then. Think of me as a novice companion."

"What can you offer me?"

"I can offer you all the gold I have."

The man crosses his arms. "No, not that. What benefit do you offer to your presence?"

"I'm a very good archer, I'm nimble, I'm the best tracker in the entire world, and I have learned a lot about the monsters of the region." She says confidently.

"I'm hunting a basilisk. Tell me about it if you know a lot."

"A basilisk… in the legends they are a large serpent with wings, but with the head of a bird."

"This isn't some legend. This is real life. What are they?"

"Let me finish! They're a large serpent with four legs, each foot is webbed for swimming and they have giant claws for climbing trees. They can live in and out of water, but most often nest near large flowing bodies of water. They are venomous, and their saliva can melt iron with ease. They can also secrete venom from their skin if being attacked."

"Anything else?" He asks with a more upbeat tone, seemingly surprised by Estelle's knowledge of basilisks.

"Well, they mostly feed from fish but have known to eat anything on land such as deer and livestock."

"Very well. You can come on this contract with me." He says as he turns and walks towards the door.

"Seriously!?" Estelle says with the utmost excitement in her voice as she follows him closely out of the guild hall's door.

"Where do you live?" He asks her with a friendly tone.

Estelle smiles and looks upward towards the stars of the night sky. "On the edge of town near the forest."

He changes his direction and walks towards the forested edge of town. "I'll walk you there."

The two walk through the snowy streets of Drixyl, seemingly enjoying each other's company through conversation, talking of the stars and the beauty of the landscape. The walk seems to only last a few seconds, even though it was nearly a twenty-minute walk.

"I'll be here at six in the morning. I prefer to travel before the paths are busy. We'll be gone for at least three days so pack what's necessary." He says as he turns and walks through the snow-covered field towards a small cabin in the distance.

"Wait!" Estelle yells out, making him stop.

"Here's your cloak back." She says as she hands him the snow-white cloak with black runes on it.

"Keep it. You'll need it for the trip." He says before turning away again.

Estelle looks towards the cabin in the distance "Is that your home?"

"Yeah." He says as he nearly disappears in the cold night air.

Estelle holds the cloak tight to her chest and returns to her home. She lights a fire in her fireplace and cooks a meal for the evening before sitting in front of the fire in her small cabin and finishing the book Johnathan gave to her before falling asleep in the comfortable beautifully crafted chair. Her home is decorated with drawings of different creatures and scenery, all signed with a large curvy 'E'. The flickering fire illuminated the rest of the front area of the cabin, in the corner is a drawing table slanted with a dozen unlit candles around it and seemingly a hundred crumpled papers thrown into a box just to the right of the table. The only sounds in the cabin are the soft breaths of Estelle who is fast asleep and the warm fire crackling softly in the fireplace.

The sun is shining in the city, people all dressed elegantly are gathered around in the middle of meticulously crafted gray stone buildings forming a circle. A man dressed in robes of purple and crown of jewels and gold stands before them holding his hands out to the crowd. Kneeling next to him with his hands tied behind his back is a man wearing a torn blue shirt and pants that are that of rags.

"Everyone, we've called you all to witness the trial of a vicious murderer. This man kneeling next to me, groveling in his own filth has been accused of murdering my son... the beloved Prince of Triveria. Your Prince! Prince Alexander Markor!" The old man says with blood lust and rage in his voice as he looks down at the man kneeling next to him. The crowd is disturbed by a loud yell and forceful push directly through the middle.

"Levi could never! He would never do such a thing! How dare you accuse him!" A woman dressed in a lilac dress with soft lavender hair nearly shoulder length and a pair of beautiful amethyst eyes is yelling as she's being pulled away from a group of Knights.

"Treason! Treason! Treason!" The old man yells. "Silence this instant you witch!"

A young woman places her hands on the shoulder of the King. "Your majesty. Father, calm down."

"I will not stand for this. Ankore! Bring her here this instant!" The King yells out to one of the knights holding the woman back.

The knight takes the woman by the arms and pulls her to the large stone stand where the King is standing with his daughter, and the man dressed in rags. "Yes, your majesty!"

"Do you understand the consequences of defending a murderer in my country, you bitch!" The King says as he raises his hand to strike the woman. "No, these are not the actions of a King."

"Good people of Triveria. Do you believe this man to be a murderer? Who has taken that which you love the most right from your hands?"

"Yes!" An ominous combined voice of the crowd yells back to the King.

"Do you wish to take something from him, as he has taken from you. That which he loves the most!?"

"Yes!" The same combined voice chants back.

"My people have spoken, criminal. Do you have any words for your beloved?"

"Amelia... I didn't..." The man kneeling tries to speak as he looks to the woman's amethyst eyes before choking on his own breath.

"Do you see, my people! A sinner has sold his tongue to the Devil! He cannot even speak for himself! Captain, her head!" The King yells.

The knight looks towards the woman he is holding captive. "Sire…" He utters under his breath in a mournful tone.

"Captain, must I repeat myself!?"

He kneels the woman down over the ledge "No sire…"

"No! Take..." The kneeling man tires to speak but cannot stop choking.

"Levi, run away! Run far away and never look back Levi!" The woman says to the man in rags as he tries to breathe. He looks into her beautiful amethyst eyes; it is as if times come to a crawl as the blade held in the knight's hand swings downward. Tears fall from her eyes. Just before the blade pierces her neck, Levi chokes again, coughing and gasping for air.

Coughing and choking he rises from is sleep, wide awake, sweating and panting. He grabs the sheets of his bed coming back to reality as he takes deep breaths.

The man with silver hair and beard lowers his head into his sweat covered hands. "It was just a dream. Just a dream…"

Chapter 2: Presage of the Wolf

A brown and black horse covered in a fur lined blanket and saddled by the man in silver and blue armor trots through the snow towards the outskirts of Drixyl. He is dressed in a black cloak, with a white rune sewn into it, aligned in the middle of his back. It is held onto his armor by two besagews with the head of a howling wolf engraved on each of them. As the sun rises over the valley, he hitches his horse outside of a small cabin just outside of Drixyl, the place Estelle calls home. He shifts through the deep snow covering the ground and shakes off the excess before stepping up to the first step. He knocks on the door three times to alert Estelle of his presence before sitting on the front step and taking an old leather notebook from his satchel. He quietly writes at a steady tempo, facing the sprawling but serene snow-covered fields waiting patiently for Estelle to emerge from her home.

Three hours pass, Estelle blinks her eyes twice as they are kissed by the sunlight. It illuminates their natural amethyst glow as she stretches. She stands and peers out of her window to the sunshine and glistening snowy fields, greeting the open valleys with a vibrant smile.

"Wait..." She stops for a moment and allows the information to register in her mind. "Fuck, I was supposed to be ready at sunrise!" She yells, hurrying to dress herself and grab all her things for her journey with the armored man she is growing fonder of.

She rushes around her home, stomping and dressing herself with one article of clothing at a time while she gathers another thing the next moment. She bursts out of her door, swinging it open forcefully.

"Did you eat?" A deep voice says from in front of her, shocking her more than the arctic chill of the outside air.

"N...no."

"Make some food, we'll be travelling all day."

"What would you like?" She asks as she drops some of her bags. The man closes his notebook and stands, grabbing her items from her.

"Nothing just makes yourself some food. I'll load your things." He says as he walks towards the horse. "Don't forget your cloak either."

She turns and walks into her house but stops abruptly for a moment. "Would you like to come in? It's freezing out here."

"No thank you." He says while loading her luggage onto his horse.

She shakes her head and returns to her home, closing the door behind her with a quick shiver. She cracks open six eggs and cuts a couple slices of fresh baked bread. While the eggs are cooking over the wood fire stove that warms her home, she finds the freshly cleaned cloak and folds it neatly on her bed.

The man returns to his post and continues writing diligently in his book, he shakes his head and scribbles a few lines out, but the familiar snap of a pencil breaking stalls his concentration.

"Damnit." He says softly to himself. He takes a knife from his leather boot and carefully sharpens the pencil to a fine point, as if he were sharpening a blade on a whetstone.

The door opens with a gentle creak and Estelle steps out into the cold morning air holding two glass plates. Each with three freshly cooked eggs and two slices of fresh bread she warmed on the stove.

"Here. You look like you're hungry." She says handing him a plate with a fork and sits down on the covered step next to him.

"Thank you." He says with a sincere appreciation as he takes in the scent of the freshly made food. He lifts his helmet's front just slightly to reveal just his mouth.

Estelle is watching with peering eyes of intensity, thinking he is going to remove his helmet. She watches him take the first bite of her food and pause for a moment, before shoveling the rest into his mouth like some sort of feral beast.

"Slow down before you choke!" She exclaims, but before she can finish her sentence, he lowers his helmet and holds the plate in his lap.

"That was delicious. Thank you again." He says turning his head towards her, noticing she hasn't even begun to eat yet. "I apologize, I should have waited to eat with you."

"No, you're okay. No need to apologize, if you're still hungry I can make you more?" She asks with a sweet smile imprinted on her cheeks.

"No, thank you. I'm full. I just haven't had such a delicious meal in a… long time." He says with a sorrowful tone as he looks towards the ground.

"What do you normally eat?"

"Normally I eat wild game that I hunt while on a contract."

"Seriously? There's a general store in town that carries, you know, normal people food, right?"

"I try to avoid going into town unless it's for business only. I'm fine surviving from the land."

"You're an odd one." She says as she takes a bite of her food. *"This isn't anything special, it's not seasoned or salted. Just plain eggs and bread.*" She thinks to herself as she eats.

The man pulls out two small metal cups from his satchel and fills them with snow and places a tea bag in each one.

"What are you doing?"

"Etin." He says under his breath. A small, palm sized flame forms in his hand. He holds the two cups over his palm for a moment, the snow melts in an instant and the leftover water comes to a quick boil in the cups. He places them in the snow for a moment and shakes the tea around, mixing them up. He feels the handle with an ungloved hand to check the temperature and hands Estelle a cup of freshly brewed tea.

"Oh… thank you. That's very handy." Her face gleaming with an intrigued expression.

"It's nice when out on a contract. No problem starting fires or heating food."

"Etin… I thought that was an offensive magic, used as an attack against enemies?"

"It is normally. But not all magic needs to be used to harm."

"Well, that's true." She says as she sips the tea. "Wow this is delicious."

"It's because of the melted snow. With normal stream water it's not nearly as pure."

"Wow." She says as she smiles and drinks the rest of her tea. "Give me your plate. We can leave now." She says with a radiant happiness in her voice as she returns the plates to her kitchen.

The man mounts his horse and waits for Estelle just near her steps. She exits her home and locks the door behind her. The man holds his black gloved hand out to help her onto the horse and lifts her on behind him.

"Don't forget the cloak." He says.

"Oh, right. Here." She says handing him the cloak.

"No, I told you to keep it. You'll need it, it'll keep you warm." He says as he helps her onto his black and brown horse.

"Can I ask you a question?"

"I guess."

"What's your name?"

He pauses for a moment and flicks the leads of his horse to guide him forward. "Lupin." He says as they trot down the snow-covered path. She smiles and looks at the back of the man who once refused to even utter his name to her.

A heavy snowfall coats the stone paths in the kingdom Triveria to the far north-east of Drixyl. The residents of the capital all settle in their homes, fireplaces stoked, and a peaceful calm has set their mind at ease once again. From over the mountains, an armored man speaks softly to himself in a foreign language. His armor is lined with a thick fur, and seemingly forged an inch thick on each piece.

"It's nearly an entire country in itself, where does it end?" The man asks himself softly, pulling his cloak across his chest.

A broad statured man approaches behind him, towering above the rest of the men. A monster in the form of a person. He is dressed in fur lined armor, dented, scratched, and stained in blood. He lifts his helm and holds it at his side, the two horns on the side nearly the length of his massive forearm.

"I'll light the signal. We will wait here for the army to arrive, and we will attack at the first nightfall after their arrival." The large blonde headed man says with snow and ice coating his long-braided beard.

"Njal, do you see the sheer magnitude of that fortress? How do you believe we will conquer this with our army? We merely number one hundred, this kingdom will raise an army ten thousand strong in a night." One of the men says, removing his helmet revealing a shaved head with old tattoos across his entire top.

"Leif, you are a direct descendent of the greatest warrior our homeland has ever known. You quiver now, at the sight of a few pebbles stacked on one-another? Look closely, Leif. This kingdom does not know war. This kingdom knows pampered hands and the suckling of a sagging teat of their mothers. We are warriors. Each man and woman of our one hundred is worth a thousand of those who have not seen war. Come, we have traveled a great distance today. We will camp and feast, I'll light the signal, you carve up the beast." Njal says valiantly, placing his hand on Leif's shoulder like a bear's paw on an ant.

"The beast?" Leif asks with a look of confusion sprawled across his face.

Njal points to a large feline creature with curved tusks pointing outward.

"I don't know what these are. It was trailing us up the mountain and it looked tasty."

"That is a daggertooth, they're not found in the homeland. Supposedly they were hunted to near extinction by our ancestors."

"I care not in the slightest. Survival means more to me than the fate of a beast."

"Aye." Leif begins to carve the carcass into thick slabs of meat and places pieces of frozen wood in the center of an area he has cleared in the thick snow. "Etin." He utters, setting the wood ablaze in an instant.

"Still playing with that black voodoo, are you? It only takes a bit of flint and a blade to start a fire."

"Aye. You should take the time to learn something other than how to kill for once. Might serve you well."

"Pfft." Njal mutters, trying to light a large bundle of sticks with flint and the blade of his axe.

"Etin!" Leif yells once again, setting the signal ablaze. The scorching fire nearly lights Njal's beard on fire. He stumbles back away and turns to Leif, glaring viciously. "Calm yourself. The food is cooking. If you fight me now, I will eat it all myself while you're unconscious." He begins to laugh, cooking the meat over the fire.

The snow from the northern regions of the realm continues its path to the southern regions of the country. Levi and Estelle are making their way to Levenwood with a steady pace as the snow begins to fall steadily over the dimly lit path where the light is slowly fading as night falls over the land.

"How far are we from Levenwood, was it?" Estelle asks.

"Not too far, just about two more hours. Are you doing alright?"

"Yes, it's starting to snow heavily, I was just curious if we'd make it there this evening."

"Have you never left Drixyl?" Lupin asks with heavy sarcasm.

"Well obviously, idiot. Do you see my ears? Do I look like I'm from Drixyl?"

"I'm not one to judge a book by its cover."

"You're incorrigible."

"Where are you from, if you don't mind me asking?"

"I'm from Fellistar, the southern elven country south of the mountain range."

"Why have you come this way then?"

"I left home about two years ago, I wanted to see the world for what it was instead of just a few trees and mountains in the distance." Estelle says with a hint of despair in her voice as she looks towards the mountains in the west with a morose glare.

"I see." He says as the conversation falls silent with the fast-approaching nightfall.

"Where are you from?" She asks in a chipper voice. But a long silence breaks her chipper smile. "What, going to play the silent game again?"

"I don't have a home, I'm from nowhere." He says with an anguished resonance in his deep voice.

"I don't believe that. Everyone has a home, where did you grow up?"

"I don't remember my childhood. It's all just a thick fog within my memories."

"What do you mean?"

"Shh. Keep your head forward, don't make eye contact with any of the people passing us by." He says as he fixes his gaze directly north.

Estelle looks around but does not see anyone in front of them. "What?"

"Shh."

A group of four men on horseback slowly approach over the hill in front of them holding torches and scouring the landscape for something it seems. One of the men in front glares towards Lupin and Estelle, locking his stare on them the closer they approach.

The men are speaking a foreign language that Estelle does not understand. She listens closely, trying to pick up a word that sounds vaguely familiar but cannot understand a word. The men are all dressed in thick gray cloaks with black and silver plate armor underneath. Their helmets are lined with fur with the face shield's cut to resemble the face of a wolf. The four men pass by Lupin and

Estelle, staring them down as if they were examining their prey upon a hunt. The men fall silent as they pass, but soon resume their conversation after they are a few trots past.

"Lupin, who were those men? I didn't understand their language, and their armor was terrifying." Estelle questions Lupin the moment the four knights are out of hearing distance.

"Triverian Elites, those were men of a scout brigade called the Fourth Edict."

"Triverian? Do you mean from the Kingdom in the north?"

"Yes. The language they were speaking is a language taught to the elite brigades to communicate freely without spies."

"What are they doing down here? This is a long way south from their Kingdom."

"If the scouts are out this far, they are looking for someone. I am sure more will be following their trail not long from now. It is best if we hurry and settle in for the evening. Once we get to Levenwood, we will set up camp in the forest and sleep until the early morning before our hunt. Keep quiet now." He says to Estelle before cracking the reigns on the horse to speed up its trot through the growing mounds of snow.

"Kristoff, that man on the horse we passed not long ago. He did not make eye contact whatsoever. Same with the girl nestled behind him. Why do you think that is?" One black armored man asks another riding next to him.

"I don't know. Perhaps he's encountered military forces before and has had an unpleasant experience."

"Maybe. They will likely rest in Levenwood for the evening. I'll contact Ankore and have him keep an eye out for any suspicious activity from the two. They should be arriving there by the morning if the weather permits."

"Do as you wish, Jeremiah. We must find a suitable place to camp this evening. The snow will soon encumber us to the point where our steeds will refuse to step any further."

"Right. Arthur! Take the lead and find a place to camp!"

"Yes sir." A deep voice thunders from the rear of the group and a black horse quickly trots past the two men in front rushing quickly down the snow-covered path.

Within the majestic castle overlooking the Kingdom of Triveria, an old pale skinned man steps slowly through the stone and wood halls of the Kingdom. He is dressed in a gold and white robe, with only a golden circlet hanging from a silver chain wrapped around his neck. The man is alone in the giant hallways, his face is being illuminated by the soft moonlight peeking through the giant windows. The sound of his footsteps echo throughout the halls, but it is as if a mouse is stepping through. He approaches a large door, one crested with gold trim and purple gemstones aligning themselves to make the Triverian symbol bestowed upon its flag. He opens the door and within the room sits an old man, with delicate white hair and a neatly trimmed beard to match. His robe is seemingly made of amethyst and gold by the way it shimmers in the moonlight.

"Your majesty." The old man dressed in gold and white speaks with a brittle voice.

"What do you desire at this hour?" The King says with a thunderous tone in the near empty room.

"The council requires your presence. Immediately."

The King of Triveria turns his gaze from the window to the old man standing in his doorway. He pauses for a moment but nods and follows the old man down the large hallways towards a staircase that looks as if it were sculpted by the hands of a god.

The old man opens a large aged oak door for the King and closes it as the King enters the room alone. Within the room lit by candle and moonlight through a skylight window stained with religious portraits, sit a circle of eight people, four men and four women. All near the age of stone with silver and white hair neatly parted one way or the other.

"Your majesty. Sit, we must discuss something of utmost importance."

"As you wish." The King sits at the open seat, directly across from the man who spoke to him.

"Your majesty. Are you aware of the impending destruction that ensues when a chosen one of the sacred loses their life?" A woman sitting next to the King asks.

"I am unaware."

"When one loses their life, the burden they carried of humanities wrong doings is released upon the world. If all six of the Sacred Knights were to be slain, it would mean the end of time. Right now, your child, who bore the mark of the Ox, every burden he carried on his shoulder for humanity is being released upon the world. Destruction and death will follow in its path."

"Dear God, how do we stop this?!" The King yells, becoming flustered for the safety of his Kingdom.

"In time, your Majesty. The man who killed your son, Levi Timeré, the Wolf. He must be brought to us immediately if we hope to stop this impending apocalypse. Soon he will strike again, he will murder another of the chosen. And then another, and another. He will not stop until he is the embodiment of evil upon this world. The demons within that man are far too powerful for any normal soldier to handle. We must purge him of this world.

Legend tells that the one who bears the Mark of the Wolf is not bestowed the power of the Gods, but the Devil. He who bears the Mark of the Wolf will be the catalyst for destruction upon the world. He who bears the Mark of the Wolf will be the end of time."

"Are you saying that Levi is planning to kill the others!? Even my daughter!? I will not stand for this!"

"Your majesty, there is only one way to stop this. He must be brought to us alive, but there is one more thing we require. Within the legend, there is a woman. She is known as the Amaranthine. The undying flower, the tamer of the Wolf. She must be found and brought here as well. Do you understand that he must be brought here alive?"

"Why!? Why should I bring him here alive!?"

"Your majesty, this man. Levi, he who bears the Mark of the Wolf. Carries the burden of humanity's worst. In legend, the Mark is known as the Demon Wolf of War. If he were to die, and his burdens be reaped upon humanity then there is no hope for the kingdom. It will fall, the people will fall, society will fall. You will fall. Do you understand?"

"Yes…" The King says under his breath. "This woman, the Amaranthine, do we know where she is?"

"We need not worry. The Devil is drawn to the soul in which he cannot reap."

"Do you mean to say that we are to just hope they find each other? How are we to capture them both?"

"Your majesty, follow me." A voice, as if the shadows whispered to the room in a low voice says.

The King stands from his chair and follows the shadowed figure through a dark hallway, as they enter torches alight with each step. The hallway seems never-ending, as if the torches appear farther and farther.

"What is this place? Why have I never seen this before?"

"This place… is of old. That of the ancient." The still shadowed figure says from the front of the king.

"This is my castle, how am I unaware of a corridor this immaculate hiding within my own halls."

"This place belongs to all who follow the word of the lord."

"That's ridiculous!"

"Silence. Through here." The figure says as they enter a room illuminated by the moonlight and a small fire pit burning blue flames. "Look around you. This is the legend of old. Decipher this and return to the council." The figure says before fading into the blue flames as if the apparition never existed.

The King stares at the flames for a moment and lights a torch with the blue flames. He steps towards the side of the room, holding the torch in front of him. Examining each piece of the stone carved legend inscribed upon the walls.

"These must be the Sacred Six of old." He says under his breath as he wipes the dust from the old stone carvings. "This must be an ancient map of the realm. These hexagons, they each bear a symbol of one of the six. Except this one here, right inside of the Kingdoms wall. This one has a different symbol." He examines all around the stone walls for a similar symbol but fails to find any sign of it. He continues down the wall. "With each death, one of the structures exudes… something. Something dark. What does this mean? What did he mean by the weight the chosen bear?" He asks himself before continuing down the wall. "The flower…" He says. "This is in ancient runes, what do they say?" He asks himself again, studying the legend with an intense mystified stare.

"They are ancient elven runes." A woman from the council says from behind the King.

"What do they say?"

"They speak of the end of times. Notice each of the chosen have died in this point of the legend. It describes the destruction of all life."

"Has this happened before?"

"Yes."

"How have we stopped the destruction in the past?"

"The Amaranthine soothes the anger dwelling within the Demon."

"So, she, the Amaranthine, must kill the Demon Wolf?"

"No, she purely makes the Demon vulnerable. The Demon must be slain by a hand of God, to stop the impending doom he will wreak upon this world."

The King moves farther down the wall, holding the blue torch high above his head to illuminate the carved wall in front of him.

"What then? After God smites the demon. What then?"

"Then the end of the danger will be upon us. The remaining of the chosen will mend the damages throughout the world. It is their duty."

"And if the demon smites them before he meets the hand of God?"

"We will summon divine protection upon the remaining chosen. They, will not suffer a death at the hands of a demon."

"Thank you, this soothes my worries for my Kingdom."

"Come, the council wishes to discuss more of the details."

The King nods and places the torch into a sconce in the corner of the room. The flickering blue flame changes to green and illuminates a soft sputtering glow upon the wall. The carvings seem to change, as if the hands of fate are meddling in the legend, or perhaps prophecy. The final carving changes entirely, revealing the Mark of the Wolf, except it holds a flower within its mouth. The flower seems to bloom into a crown upon the wolf's head as the green flame flickers into a dim nothingness and the room falls dark and silent.

Early in the morning, a slow rising sun illuminates the dark snow-covered forest outside of Levenwood. The river flows steadily through the frozen forest from the mountain hot springs of Lake Niroh in the rocky cliffs above. The source water is keeping the river from freezing entirely and making it lukewarm to the touch. Lupin has built a shelter from the thick snow and ice to conceal their location from their suspected beast. Lupin has tied a small deer to the base of a tree as bait for their hunt, the adolescent deer is snorting and grunting as it tries to free itself from the rope wrapped carefully around its shoulders.

"Is it not cruel to use live bait?"

"Live bait means a quick contract. The temperature will drop quickly by the water, and metal armor does not pair well with the cold. If we're out here for too long even the lining and cloaks won't save us from the weather."

"I understand that, but this just seems cruel."

"Hunting monsters cannot rely on the morals of intelligent life. It is a fight for survival on this path, I must follow the rules of the ancient world to stay alive."

"The morals of intelligent life?"

"Shh." Lupin hushes Estelle and peeks his head out of the small shelter he has built. "It's coming for breakfast."

The large serpentine creature creeps through the water like a predator, swimming silently as its gaze is locked upon its prey. The deer has calmed down and is drinking from the river, unaware of the beast peering at it from the water. The serpentine monster dips underwater, readying itself for a quick and easy kill. Lupin steps from their shelter silently, as if he is a predator stalking his prey. He creeps slowly to a large tree near the water, only a few feet from where the deer is drinking. He watches carefully at the ripple within the icy water, waiting for his opportunity to strike. He unsheathes his sword from the scabbard attached neatly to his armor. Estelle peeks from the shelter, curious to what is about to unfold just before her eyes.

"I've never seen an actual monster hunt before. I've only read of them, yet this is nothing like I've read." She says softly to herself as she intently watches Lupin wait like a statue.

The deer lifts its head from the water and steps back slowly and cautiously, aware that danger is lurking in the water. Just as the deer takes its second step back, the basilisk lunges from the icy water, jaws wide open towards the deer's throat. In a split second before the jaws of the basilisk immobilize the deer and drag it into the icy depths of the river, a razor-like blade slices through the soft unprotected section of the basilisk's throat, right where it bends its neck. Blood splatters on the snow ground, causing the snow to melt in the precise scarlet red spots. The basilisk's body falls to the ground as if a boulder just fell from a mountain. Its body slides a few feet before coming to a complete stop in the snow. Lupin watches carefully as the acidic saliva melts a rock directly in front of the beast's body like a hot knife slicing through butter. Estelle's jaw drops as she watches from the shelter, trying to comprehend how easily Lupin had just slain a beast that is notorious in legend for being a serious threat to an entire brigade of soldiers, and he was able to slay it with purely one precise strike with his sword.

Lupin releases the deer that was tied to the tree and steps on the severed head of the Basilisk just below the start of the jawbone. The remaining saliva squirts from the opening in the next and onto the ground, eating away at the snow and soil. Estelle steps form the shelter and approaches Lupin with the same look of surprise on her face. Lupin takes a rope from his waist pouch and ties the severed head carefully not to touch the excess saliva and carries it back towards the shelter, now realizing Estelle has left the shelter.

"Why are you out of the shelter?" He asks.

"It's over, what's the big deal?"

"You don't know if it's over. Just because one was slain doesn't mean another isn't lurking in the distance."

"Basilisks are known to live in solitude, they have never been known to travel in pairs."

"It does not matter. Stay in the shelter until I return, that is the rule."

"How am I to learn anything if I'm just to stay in the shelter!?" She yells, now becoming flustered with the difficulty of Lupin, he walks past her and enters the shelter leaving the severed head outside. She follows behind him and returns to her spot where they waited prior. The two remain silent for a little while before it's broken by Lupin's deep voice.

"What was that look for?" He asks.

"What look?"

"You looked as if you'd just seen a specter. Why so surprised?"

"Oh, I've never witnessed anything like that before."

"Like what?"

"How you killed it, the entire hunt honestly. Everything I've read said that basilisks proposed a serious threat even to a brigade of soldiers, but you handled it as if it were some simple prey."

"Knowledge keeps you alive when taking contracts, basilisks are serious threats to those who are ignorant. Are you familiar with the scale that monsters are rated on?"

"No, I'm not familiar. What is it?"

"It's simple. A scale from one to ten, one being minimal danger, ten being a serious enough danger to cripple an entire city."

"Okay, simple enough. Where does a basilisk fall?"

"Between a five and six depending on size and age. The older they are the more dangerous they become. That was a younger female, so I'd say a five. If it had gotten it's bearing on land, I would have been in danger, but I was able to strike its softened nape before it landed, that's ideal. When they are on land or water, they keep their head low covering the soft skin underneath. The reason they are considered dangerous throughout legend is because of that, most will try to get the beast on land, thinking they'll have the advantage, but even an experienced warrior would have serious difficulty taking care of the contract in that scenario."

"How did you learn so much about monsters? I've read every book available, but nothing mentioned any of that."

"It's because those books were written by those who haven't experienced the beast in person. Most are scholars who just rewrite material from previous books and change a couple words to make it seem different."

"I noticed you writing outside of my cabin, are you writing a book of monsters?"

"Something like that."

"Well, that's fantastic. I think it will be a great book."

"It's partially something my father was working on. He was an explorer, a man of science who never backed down from any challenge or adversity when traveling. He had the thought that these monsters were nothing different than your average cattle, that with proper understanding we could stop eradicating these beasts from the world."

"Your father sounds very smart. I'm sure he's happy you've taken on his work."

"Yeah, maybe. He was the best."

"Was? Oh, Lupin I'm sorry." Estelle says with sorrow in her voice, reaching towards Lupin.

Lupin nods his head as Estelle squeezes his hand. "It's alright. He passed when I was young."

"How old were you?"

"I don't know, I was barely thirteen if I remember correctly."

"Thirteen? Wow, have you been alone the entire time since then?"

"Sort of. I have had friends, but my mother died at birth. When my father passed, another family took me in, though it was never the same. All I have left that was his, is this pendant." Lupin pulls a silver pendant with a howling wolf engraved into it from under his tunic. "He gave it to me the last time he and I were together."

"I'm so sorry, Lupin. I know it is not easy losing loved ones. How long have you been traveling alone?"

"Six months or so. Not long."

"Only six months? I assumed you were alone for a lot longer. You're so... seasoned, I guess." Estelle grins.

Lupin nods with a chuckle. "I guess I've seen a thing or two in my travels."

"I hope we can do this more often. Though I did not contribute, this was interesting. Oh, and you should try to do that more." She smiles.

Lupin turns his head towards Estelle with a slight confusion in his voice. "Do what?"

"Talk, laugh, maybe even let me see if you can smile." Estelle chuckles, nudging Lupin with her foot.

Lupin chuckles a little. "I'll see what I can do, let's get some sleep, we'll travel in the night to avoid any unnecessary interaction with people."

"Okay that's a good idea, I'm exhausted from staying up all night."

In Levenwood, a large platoon of knights fifty strong are waiting outside of an inn they had commandeered the night prior. The men are lined into squads facing the dirt road running through the town.

"Men, our scouts are arriving at the town of Drixyl this morning. We have information that the criminal in question is residing in this town. We will advance at once; the scouts are setting up shelter on the southern outskirts of the town. Do not forget why we are on this journey. I hand selected each of you men for the sole reason of your loyalty to the King. The criminal was a dear friend to each one of us, but his treason must outweigh each of our desires to side with him. He is extremely skilled, extremely clever, and extremely dangerous. Do not fight him alone, never break away from your squad, and use your Triverian star sapphire communication stones to communicate to everyone in the platoon, no other stone is permitted to be used. This way we can ensure that our communication is secure, do I make myself clear?"

"Yes Captain!" The entire platoon yells.

"Very good. Now we will be active in the early morning and through the night only. Our information states that is when he has been seen and he hides during the daytime. Not many people in the town know of his presence and he has made no attempts to find aid within the town. Be aware, though our information is clear, it may not be fully correct. Assume everyone in the town to be conspiring against our will, demand information and demand cooperation. Our first foot into town will be tonight after sundown, until then we will rest until our time has come. Am I understood?"

"Yes Captain!" The entire platoon yells in excitement.

"Very good. Triveria be with us!"

"HAAA!" The platoon chants back.

"Squad leaders. Ready your men, we leave immediately!"

"Yes, Captain Ankore!" The squad leaders yell back.

Captain Ankore is the first to mount his horse, he turns and looks down the snow-covered dirt path ahead of them.

"Levi, the time has come for us to reunite. Perhaps we will meet again in the afterlife, brother." He says softly before placing his helmet upon his head. He holds his wrist to the mouth opening in his helmet and a green gemstone illuminates dimly.

"We're leaving for Drixyl now. We will be there soon, any sightings of the criminal this morning?" He says softly into the gemstone.

A soft female voice chimes through the green gemstone. "He will return from a contract this evening. Be aware of the master of the guild."

Captain Ankore lowers his wrist and begins his journey down the snow-covered path. The platoon of men follows behind him. Fifty plus men thunder down the snow-covered path with the scent of vengeance and an eerie bloodlust trailing behind them as if their long journey is destined to come to an end.

Chapter 3: The Raven's Burrow

Lupin and Estelle are nearing the outskirts of Drixyl, the freezing night air has brought a steady snowfall from northern Lake Neroh southbound and the already frozen ground is growing with a consistent uprising towards the sky. Lupin draws his horse to a stop as they arrive at Estelle's cabin.

"This is where we part ways for the day."

"Don't you have to return to the guild hall?"

"I do, but it is late. I plan to return to my cabin right after, the weather delayed our trip far longer than I anticipated. Go in and get some actual rest and eat. I'll see you around."

"Do you wish to stay for dinner? I can make something for you, it has been a few days since we left. A nice home cooked meal would be nice."

"No, thank you for the offer though. The streets get dangerous at night." He says as she dismounts the horse.

"When am I going to see you again?"

Lupin pulls the reins of his horse towards the dirt road. "Next time I take a contract I'll be sure to include you.". Estelle smiles and feels a warm feeling emerge from her body. She takes her things and enters her home for the evening. Lupin continues into town but hitches his horse just on the outskirts before entering. "You'll be safe here." He whispers before throwing a thick blanket over the horse's back.

He makes his way through town with the tied head of the basilisk in his hand, he walks carefully through the alleyways watching every corner and every person he passes by.

"I am back a little earlier than I would have liked to be, hopefully the guild hall is empty." He thinks to himself as he swiftly traverses the town's road. He approaches the guild hall and opens the large oak door. *"Great, still not empty, but this is busier than normal for this time."*

"Did you see the knights arrive this morning? There must have been fifty of them." A woman says to her counterparts at one of the guilds tables.

"Yes. I watched them as they came here. A few arrived earlier than the rest and set up camp on the southern outskirts. I find it odd that Triverian soldiers are down here in our little slice of Senary. They must be trailing someone to come down this far, and that many."

"That's exactly what I was thinking."

"Great. Time to get moving again, I knew I've stayed here far too long." Lupin says to himself quietly as he pushes through the crowd towards

Johnathan's office. A knight dressed in black cumbersome armor with the Triverian star on his breastplate watches from the corner of the room, examining every person that enters and leaves the hall. He raises his wrist to his mouth for a moment then back down again before exiting the guild hall.

Johnathan closes the door behind Lupin. "You're back sooner than I had thought, I was prepared to stay up late today."

"I did not intend to be back this early. It seems I have lost track of time."

"I see you completed the contract, any difficulty?"

"None to mention."

"Same as usual then, here's your gold. Listen, there is a group of Triverian Knights camped just outside of Drixyl, do you know anything of this?" Johnathan asks inquisitively as he hands him two gold coins.

"I have no affiliation."

"Levi. I am not an idiot. You came here half a year ago out of nowhere. You clearly have strong prowess with a sword, your mannerisms are nothing of some commoner, you travel alone, and only come early or late. Clearly you are hiding from a past, or perhaps a future." Johnathan says in a calming tone to Levi.

"Johnathan. You have become a trusted friend to me, I do not wish for you to become involved in my affairs. Anyone who does will be in immediate danger. I will be leaving town this evening and I will continue my journey on the path. I ask two things from you, my friend."

"Anything, Levi."

"When you see the elven woman whom I traveled with on this contract, Estelle. Tell her I left town for the south and I will not be back, and if any of the Triverian Knights question you of affiliation with me. Tell them you do not have any, insist I was nothing more than common rabble with a social problem."

"Levi, that girl is infatuated with you. She waited day and night for you just to ask you to come on a contract."

"I understand that, but... it is not safe. I am not sure I will even be able to keep myself alive past these next few evenings. I am not willing to let them take another life because of my failures. I have managed to stay far enough ahead of the Triverian army for quite some time, but I have let myself become comfortable and I do not want anyone here to suffer for my ignorance." Levi says, staring at Johnathan, who sits back in his chair and ponders in silence for a moment, examining the man sitting before him.

"Alright Levi. Where will you truly be going?"

"I don't know, but as far away as I can get." Levi says before counting out one hundred gold pieces from his pouch. Johnathan watches as Levi counts out a small fortune from his pouch. "Give these to Estelle when you see her tomorrow. Tell her to buy some equipment and books."

"Levi, that's more than a year's wage for the average person in Senary, are you serious?"

"Yes. Just ensure she takes it. She can be quite a handful."

"I will, my friend."

A strong knock breaks the tender farewell of the two friends followed by a thunderous voice from just outside the oak door.

"Johnathan Ryker, Master of the Guild of Drixyl. I require your presence this instant. I am Captain Theodore Ankore of the Triverian Army Special Forces." The Captain says from just outside of the door.

Johnathan looks to Levi and quickly writes a note on a small piece of paper. He hands it to Levi before swinging the large bookshelf in his room outward revealing a narrow pathway out of the building.

"Run." He whispers to Levi before closing the bookshelf behind him.

"Johnathan Ryker! Open this door this instant, or I will use force to remove you from behind it!" Captain Ankore's thunderous voice booms from outside of the door. Johnathan swings the door open wide with a charismatic smile and cheerful posture.

Johnathan looks towards the Captain with an informal expression, as if they had been friends for years. "Good evening, Cap'. What can I do for you this evening?".

The Captain removes his helmet and stares him in the eyes viciously. His face is scarred alongside of his brow down to his cheek. His helmet at his side is similar to the other knights accompanying him, though his helmet bears a silver Triverian star and three small golden circles surrounding the star, signifying his rank among the soldiers.

The Captain holds a hand drawn poster of a young man, completely resembling Levi. "Nice to meet you, Johnathan Ryker. We are here by order of the King searching for a criminal, wanted for treason, adultery, theft, and murder of the Prince. Do you recognize him, his name is Levi Timeré?"

Johnathan examines the poster carefully. "Treason, murder, adultery, and theft!? By Gods, this man must be captured. Good Captain, the first hint that I hear of the whereabouts of this dastardly man I will ensure you are notified immediately!" Johnathan says in a sincere tone.

"Johnathan. I wish to make something concise. My men will be hanging these wanted signs all around your fine hall and all around Drixyl. If a single one is torn down…I will know." Captain Ankore leans forward into Johnathan's face close enough that Johnathan can see the red veins in his eyes. "And I will punish the person who does for aiding the criminal. I have authorization from the King to use direct capital punishment to any who commits a crime against the Kingdom. Do I make myself clear?"

"Yes. I understand. Do not remove the posters."

The Captain places his helmet back on and turns to the main door of the hall. "Good. Then we are off." Before he and his men exit, he turns to Johnathan once more. "Oh, and before I forget, Mr. Ryker. If I find that you were lying to me. You will be publicly punished for aiding the criminal. I promise you the punishment will be severe, and I will learn the truth one way or another. I hope we will not have an altercation, but I am not above doing things a normal man might…wince to. Do I make myself clear?"

"I understand. Have a good evening, Cap'." Johnathan says with the same charismatic smile as the platoon of knights leave the guild hall. He examines one of the posters hanging from the wall in the hall. "*Oh dear, Levi, what in the world have you gotten yourself into. Hopefully, Isabella can be of more assistance than I can."* He thinks to himself as the remaining guild members watch in silence from their seats.

As the snow falls steadily over the still land, Levi is sprinting through the deep snow as fast as he can heading northwest from town.

"Isabell Ryker, Lord of Vorchid. Fuck, fuck, fuck. This is cutting it way too close. I do not have a choice; I am going to have to run all night. I cannot even slow down. Fuck! My horse is still hitched outside. Ah, no matter. Estelle can keep the horse." He shouts as he tries to pace himself for the long run ahead of him. "Damnit, I told Estelle I've been traveling alone for the past six months. If she lets that information slip out, she will be in over her head with the knights. " Levi sighs. "Only time will tell."

All through the night, the warrior led astray by fate, ran as fast and hard as his body could manage. The snow piled as far as the eye could see with near no end in sight as a white out blizzard took over the already pearly white fields. In the distance he could see a dim flickering pair of torches signifying an entrance, yet he could not decipher if the lights were merely an illusion of his fatigue. He pushed his limits as far as he could and beyond, finding strength he was unaware he had through pure determination to keep enduring forward.

Captain Ankore approaches the camp where his platoon of soldiers calls their temporary home, a distinct hint of disdain radiates from him with each step he takes. The moment his armor-clad boot steps inside of the makeshift shelter housing each of the men, they all come to a saluted stand, giving respect to their leader.

"Calm down everyone, we need not hold formalities such as this in our camp. Take your seats." He calmly says to his platoon of subordinates, setting a relaxed tone throughout the camp. "I've just spoken to my informant here in Drixyl, she is unaware of the criminal's current whereabouts, though the master of the guild was far too casual with me, as if he were performing a play. My informant has given me the information I need to apprehend the guild's master. In the early morning, we will march through the streets with our flags held high and apprehend the criminal's accomplice. We will hold a public trial for him, destroying his reputation, and giving the people of this town a glimpse of what I am willing to do if someone commits an act of treason against the Kingdom. Any objections?" The Captain says confidently to his soldiers. A Lynx man, five-eleven in height, with pampered black and white fur stands from the rear of the camp.

"I have, but one objection sir."

"Kristoff, of all the men in this platoon, I would never assume you to defy my will."

"I wish for justice to be served to all who commit travesties against the Kingdom, Captain.

But justice comes with the proper justification of a crime. What information do you have stating that the master of this guild has taken side with the criminal?"

"I have a signed scripture from the master to the criminal, informing him of Triverian Army soldiers advancing towards Drixyl."

Kristoff's ears twitch as he grows curious, a common action of members of the Lynx race. "May we see the scripture?"

"No, this information is above your rank."

"On whose authority?"

Captain Ankore stomps viciously towards Kristoff, alarming the entire platoon. "On my authority! Do I make myself clear, Kristoff?"

"Yes Captain." Kristoff says with a scheming glare towards the Captain before returning to his seat.

"Any more objections!?" The Captain yells, with a powerful shout to his platoon. "Good, Kristoff, take your fellow scouts and make rounds through the evening. We need a steady perimeter setup and a detailed map of all pathways the criminal could take throughout the town. Now."

"May we finish our meal first?" Kristoff asks.

"Now!"

"Yes, Captain." Kristoff says, standing along with his fellow members of his scout squad. Placing his blackened helmet resembling a wolf upon his head and wrapping a black cloak around his armor with the mark of Triveria in gold inlay on the back.

"Do not return until you have fully completed the tasks in great detail." The Captain says before leaving the campsite and returning to his private tent.

"Come on. I do not wish to remain here, bring your food with you." Kristoff says to his fellow scouts.

Kristoff and his squad leave the camp and mount their horses, with a swift pull of the reigns the horses all dart towards town.

In the Kingdom of Triveria, the room housing the legend of old begins to flicker with a red glow, as if the devil were rolling the dice of fate upon the world's destiny. The stone carved legend begins to change and augment itself once again, the wolf with the crown of flowers has now taken the flower back into its teeth, and the pedals of the flower begin to wilt and decay as if the stone itself were crumbling before the red glow of the torches on the wall.

"I see, so the legend does change. Just as I had thought." A shadowed figure only seen between the flickering of the red glow says in an ominous voice. "Perhaps the hands of fate play a role in the legend of old, continually changing as history writes itself time and time again. Good."

The figure says before disappearing into the shadows as if it were never there to begin with.

"Did you hear that?" A woman in a hooded gold and white silk robe says to the others dressed in the same robe, all sitting around a large stone table.

"Yes, perhaps the apparition has returned once again, now that the legend has been set into motion."

"The Demon Wolf, will he guide the hands of fate, or will the dice roll against him."

"We must pray that God smites the devil from his place in this world."

"I do not believe we can rely on God; we are merely his creation; it is not his duty to protect those who sin."

"We are his chosen vessels, we are judgment, we are the remaining of the ancient. We will decide where the dice land."

"The King has sent a platoon of soldiers to find the Wolf, and the Amaranthine. I do not believe they will be successful."

"Why do you say this?" The group answers together to a hooded man standing in the corner of the room, with the gold trim of his robe shimmering in the moonlight.

"The Wolf is no mere common man. The Wolf is the embodiment of all evil within the world, the devil in the body of a man. Do we believe a few soldiers are able to handle someone who is known throughout history as the devil?"

"I believe these soldiers will fulfill their duty, without fail." The woman says as she stands from her seat.

"You are a fool, the devil does not concede to the will of man, nor the will of God. The devil is the being in which the hands of fate may not touch, nor the roll of the dice will dismay. The devil is the being who crippled the structures of humanity, and brought upon creatures of hell, we have made mild

peace with the being we refer to as demi-humans.

But they are all the same, no different than the

creatures that haunt our villages and roam our

lands. Humanity will fall, the kingdom will fall, we

will fall. The devil will bring humanity to its knees

and destroy all that we know. The devil is more

powerful than you have ever known." The man says

as he moves from the shadows, removing his hood

and revealing his old sagging face. His face is

burned, as if he were branded like cattle. "This is

the reality of a fallen kingdom, a fallen king. A

demon gave me this mark as he crippled my

kingdom. He was slain by the hand of God, but

God... God is no longer with us in this world. God

is dead." The man says, placing his hood back

above his head as he struggles to walk towards the

long dark hallway only illuminated by a few

flickering torches. The group sitting around the

table all turn to each other once more.

"We must stop the demon, if Lord Doric's words bear any truth, then we are in much more danger than we had originally thought. The Wolf must be brought to us with the Amaranthine. If he cannot be brought here, we must force him here. It is time to begin the prophecy. The legend will guide our light's way."

"Yes. Let us begin." The group says in an eerie synchronous voice.

All eight of the gold and white robed people sitting around the table place their hands flat on the table, in a slow tempo, they begin to chant. Their hands are all old, weathered, and wrinkled. A white light appears in the middle of the table, forming a rune, growing brighter with each chant. The rune forms a hexagon, illuminating brighter at each of the corners, as if they are activating something in a sequence. The light becomes brighter than the surface of the sun, before suddenly dispersing into nothing but a few sparkling pieces of physical mana.

"The prophecy has begun…" The old man who stepped into the hallway says as he stares into the room of the stone carved legend. A white light has appeared on the stone wall at the very beginning over the Mark of the Ox.

All through the night, Levi ran as hard as he could. The snow covered the ground as if the mountains of heaven were shattered with an avalanche. As his fatigued and dehydrated body steps closer and closer to the gates of Vorchid, where the two torches had illuminated his path through the night, he loses consciousness and falls to the ground just before reaching the gate. Two guards standing with halberds at the single foot gate of Vorchid watch as the struggling man falls to the ground, unsure if he is alive or dead, and uncaring in either matter. Without a single hint of worry, they replant their eyes forward towards the snow-covered dirt path and continue their duty of guarding the city's gate.

"What are you two doing!? Help him!" A brunette woman with ample bust says as she leaves her home and wraps herself in a thick sequin cloak lined with fur. The men do not give her any attention, and keep their post held strong. "You two are ridiculous!" She yells as she runs past the guards and towards Levi who lay unconscious on the ground.

The woman takes his hand and looks towards the guards, who refuse to look back at her. With a quick scoff, she shakes her head and tries to drag Levi through the snow back to her home. She struggles endlessly, as Levi, covered from head to toe in steel plate armor is much too heavy for her to move. The woman turns to both men, and stares at each of them for a moment.

"Ah, Dohere." She says with a wave of her fingers. A green willow encumbers the two men and they drop their weapons at their feet. "Take him to my home, lay him on the sofa."

Both men obey her will and lift Levi onto their shoulders, carrying him across the small stone bridge and into the home of the mysterious brunette woman. She follows them, holding her fingers at an awkward position, almost in the shape of a rune. The two men set him down on the sofa and stand with their hands at their sides, seemingly ready for another order.

"Return to your posts." She says confidently with an arrogant smile. The men leave the home, closing the door behind them. The woman returns her hand to a normal posture and shakes her hand as if she had a cramp. "I could get use to that; bossing people around is kind of fun." She chuckles and walks towards Levi who is unconscious, still breathing heavily on the sofa. "What in the world are you?" She asks the unconscious man laying before her. She unstraps his helmet and lifts it from his head. Silver hair falls over his blotchy red face where the unfrozen sweat has completely dispersed. She stands and stumbles backwards nearly falling over the low table in the center of the room, holding her hand over her mouth. "Levi…" She says to herself softly as a smile creeps through her surprise and her face is illuminated with a wondrous joy.

Chapter 4: The Guild's Pendant

The next morning, Levi rises at the crack of dawn, just as the sun shines through the windows of the home he has awoken in. He looks around for a moment trying to understand what is going on. In a panic he leaps to his feet, realizing his armor has been removed and he is in just his undergarments. The smell of fresh cooked meat and baked bread draw him like a hungry predator towards easy prey. He carefully steps towards the origin of the scent, slowly and quietly. He takes one step into the next room and is halted by the sight of the mysterious brunette woman, as if he had seen a ghost.

"Oh, Levi. You're finally awake." She says with a kind smile and bright hazel eyes shimmering in the sunlight.

A shocked expression overcomes Levi's cautious composure, and his body relaxes as his eyes widen in excitement. "Maria..."

As the sun rises over the tree line in Drixyl, Estelle awakes, excited for the day ahead of her. She prepares a meal in haste and an extra one in a wooden container wrapped in a cloth. She readies her things and emerges from her warm cabin into the brisk mountainous snowy fields that appeared overnight. With a smile she wraps the cloak given to her by the man she knows as Lupin around her shoulders and treads through the deep snow with a skip in her step. With joy in her walk, she makes her way into town, the streets are relatively empty, although she notices that a horse is hitched outside of the outskirts of town on a nearby fence.

"Hey, that is Lupin's horse." She says to herself with curiosity as she makes her way past.

Through the town she frolics with a joyous smile that could brighten the day even under the gloomiest of skies. She comes to an immediate halt as she arrives at the guild hall, noticing the yellowed paper hanging from the door. She examines it with piercing eyes for a moment.

"A criminal of the Kingdom? Huh, odd to see wanted posters around here. Maybe the knights Lupin and I passed by the other day posted this. Long silver hair, early twenties, with deep blue eyes, huh that's how the attendant at the medical building described Lupin." She shrugs and swings the door open with a joyous smile.

The guild hall is rather quiet for the time, though Estelle pays no mind to it. She takes a seat at one of the small wooden tables, humming a tune and begins reading the book that Johnathan had given her a few days ago. Johnathan emerges from his office with sharp caution, with a few quick glances around the hall.

He sees Estelle sitting at the table alone reading and swaying her legs back and forth. "Estelle. Please come to my office." He says with a professional tone, though with a great deal of caution in his voice, before shutting the door behind him.

Estelle does not think much of Johnathan's tone and picks up her things. Estelle skips through the hall towards his office.

"Good morning, sir. What can I do for you today, have you seen Lupin by chance?"

"Lupin?"

"Oh, I guess I should not say his name so nonchalantly, it is kind of a big deal that he told me." She says with an aloof smile, and upbeat tone.

"Estelle, take a seat. I have something to give you." He says, reaching under his desk and taking a large canvas sack of coins out from under it. "This is from your…friend. He instructed me to give it to you to purchase gear and books."

Estelle takes the large heavy sack and a look of confusion overcomes her smile. "Is this from Lupin?"

"I… assume so." Johnathan says, not understanding why she is referring to Levi as Lupin. Estelle opens the sack and her jaw drops in an immediate shock.

"Sir, I cannot take this… this is a fortune."

"I was instructed to give it to you. Please just take it and listen to your friend."

"Sir, what happened to Lupin."

"Ah, Estelle. You're a sweet girl, but can I hold trust within you?"

"Yes, you can trust me sir. What happened to him?"

"He's gone south, and he will not be coming back."

"South? Why south?"

"This is all he told me."

Estelle looks at Johnathan with smoldering curiosity for a moment, not believing his words for a single second.

"Then I'll go south too."

"No!" Johnathan says as he stands. "It's not safe. There is a criminal on the loose, please just stay right here."

"I cannot do that. Lupin promised me that he will find me whenever he takes another contract. If he went south on a contract, then he broke the promise. That's not something I take lightly; I will not stand for that."

"Estelle, please."

Estelle stands from her seat and swinging the door open and with each step she takes, an ever-growing anger overcomes her. "Goodbye, Johnathan."

Before she makes it to the door, Captain Ankore barges in through the heavy oak doors, nearly knocking Estelle over with the swing.

"Johnathan Ryker! I demand your presence immediately!" The Captain yells, nearly shaking the entire guild hall to the ground. Johnathan emerges from his office once more, with minor hesitation, though he still wears the same charismatic smile in the face of the authority figure standing before him.

"What can I do for you today, Cap.?" Johnathan says as he extends his hand for a handshake.

Captain Ankore grabs Johnathan's extended arm and pulls it behind him, tying his hands together, causing Johnathan to wince with the pain.

"What are you doing!? I have done nothing wrong!" Johnathan yells.

"Johnathan Ryker. I gave you strict orders that if you aided the criminal, there would be public punishment served under the authority of the King. I have a handwritten letter to Levi warning him of our presence here, signed with your signature. This is an act of treason against the King, you are guilty of aiding the criminal and deterring justice from being served!" The Captain yells.

"I did no such thing! I have written no letter! I demand to see this letter; it is surely a fake!" Johnathan yells.

"QUIET!" Captain Ankore screams into Johnathan's ear before throwing him to the ground and kicking him in the head, knocking him unconscious with the heavy steel wrapped around the front of his boot.

"Stop that!" Estelle yells. "Our guild master did no such thing; he is a kind man!" Estelle yells standing a few steps away from the Captain.

"Your master is a criminal. He will be punished this afternoon. I only wish to keep the Kingdom and all the people of Senary safe. Now silence, before you endure similar punishment for deterring justice from being served!" Captain yells, startling Estelle. "Men take him to the town square. Build the gallows immediately, rip the wood from the buildings if you must." Captain Ankore beckons to the knights standing at the door.

"Yes Captain!" One of the armored knights says energetically as he lifts Johnathan over his shoulder and shuffles out of the guild hall.

"Young woman, I will hold a public trial for this suspected criminal at noon. I demand all residents of this town to be present. Spread the word." Ankore says, as Estelle stares at him with a fury unbeknown to her prior to this as he walks out of the door.

Estelle clutches her items tightly against her chest. *"Lupin... where are you."* "Wait, his horse. He did not leave yet! Maybe he is still in his cabin!" She exclaims, bursting through the oak door and sprinting through the snow streets towards the northern fields of Drixyl where Levi's cabin sits alone.

She approaches the cabin, nearly gasping for breath because the icy winter air feels like blades piercing her lungs. She swings the door open wide, noticing there is no lock on the door whatsoever. She steps into the cold, dark and unfurnished cabin.

"Lupin! Lupin, are you here!?" She exclaims in desperation.

Estelle makes her way to the opening in the back of the cabin, where a bedroom lies open with only a single bed and fur blanket atop of it. She rips the blanket off the bed, a small thud across the room startles her momentarily.

"What is this?" She asks herself and only the shadows in the room. She picks up a small black notebook that's pages are aged dearly along with the leather backing. Opening the notebook, her eyes light up with a distinct look of curiosity. Quickly she flips through the weathered pages of the notebook skimming each page as fast as she can. Suddenly she stops on a page near the end of the notebook.

"I've decided to take Estelle on the next contract with me, she's a handful, but she's smart. Perhaps she can be of some assistance to me with some training. I cannot quite decipher the meaning, but it is as if I am drawn to her. I don't understand the meaning, nor the feeling but perhaps this is where the hands of fate are pushing me." She reads aloud, blushing slightly as her eyes dart back and forth across the old notebook's pages. *"She's going to ask my name; I can already tell. I cannot involve her in my affairs, perhaps a moniker would appease her and keep my identity hidden."* She continues. *"I've stayed here for too long I feel, perhaps it is time to move on, though I've enjoyed this quiet little town it will not be long before the Triverian army becomes a danger to all the people of this town. We shall see. Signed, **Levi Timeré**"*.

Estelle closes the notebook and quietly thinks to herself for a moment. "I knew it, I knew it! Lupin was such a stupid name! I knew it! Damn idiot! Why not come find me!? I would have helped you run!? I knew it!" She yells in the empty cabin.

"There's nothing in here to even break! How can I be mad at him and not break a vase of his or something!" Estelle slows her breathing and begins to calm down. She places the notebook into her satchel and storms out of the cabin.

"Okay, clearly he didn't go south. His horse is still here and traversing the mountain paths with this much snow would be far too difficult. He left in a hurry if he left his notebook too. Johnathan knows more than he let on, I need to get to him before the knights throw him in a cell." Estelle says wrapping her cloak around her and running towards town once again.

Captain Ankore watches as a squad of his soldiers demolish a storefront to build gallows for the public trial of Johnathan Ryker. Three men demolish the storefront, while two others work steadily for building. Kristoff and his squadron of scouts approach the Captain from the rear, watching as they destroy a town's store for the sake of an execution.

"Captain. We have no signs of any escape of the criminal, do you wish to set up a perimeter around the town?"

"Yes. Take the rest of the platoon and post two to three soldiers at every exit in the town. Assign the others to scour the town for anyplace he may be hiding. Use force if necessary."

"Yes Captain." Kristoff says with an obedient tone before turning and walking away.

"Lieutenant Kristoff. Come here for a moment."

"Yes, Captain."

"I have received word that the criminal must be brought alive, along with an elven woman. This is a direct order from the King, though I do not agree with it. If possible, take him alive, if not, then so be it. But, be sure to thoroughly torture him prior to his death for his acts of villainy against the

Kingdom. Hold any elven woman you find hostage and bring them to me; it may be a way to lure him in if he has some sort of connection to her."

"What does the elven woman look like?" Kristoff asks.

"It does not matter, round up all of them. They're all rubbish just like the other half human hybrids."

"Captain, I ask you kindly to watch your tone."

"Go, unless you prefer to suffer as the criminal will." The Captain scoffs as he continues his direct supervision over the construction.

"Yes, Captain." Kristoff says with a slight hesitation and an expression full of anger. He places his helmet atop his head and turns swiftly down the stone path through town.

Kristoff stops in front of the three men dressed in similar armor to him. Their helmets all differ slightly, with their ranks embedded on the side. Kristoff being the highest rank of the four. He bears the Triverian star with two golden bars directly underneath. "Scouts, we have new orders. Search the town, round up any elven women you find and bring them to the captain as well. They must be brought alive."

"Kristoff why are we rounding up elven women, if you don't mind me asking?" the slender scout dressed in a black armor and a cloak to match asks.

"Jameson, it is the orders of our captain. He wishes to bait Levi with them, hoping he has a significant connection to one."

"That is absurd. We're scouts for the proud Triverian army, why are we holding innocent townsfolk hostage."

"Jameson, I wish not to bicker back and forth about this. Do as you wish, but it will be our heads if the captain's wishes are not fulfilled. Turn over every stone, check every closet, thoroughly search every potential hiding place within this town."

"Yes, sir." Jameson hesitates as the other two members of the scout's nod in agreement with Kristoff's orders from their captain.

The group of knights dressed in black armor rummage through the town thoroughly and efficiently, ripping apart homes, storefronts, restaurants, and everything in between. One knight, who is larger than the rest in stature, yet whose footsteps are as light as an assassin gathers the women throughout the town and brings them to the town square, where the gallows are nearly finished.

"Good, tie their hands on the scaffolding of the gallows at once. Cover their mouths as well, I do not wish to hear their wines and cries throughout the afternoon." Captain Ankore demands from the scout.

"As you wish, Captain." He answers with obedience.

He ties them all to the scaffolding and covers their mouths with a soft piece of cloth wrapped tightly around their heads.

"Captain, what about that one? I did not see her throughout our search." The scout asks, pointing to Estelle who is wrapped in Levi's cloak walking through the streets of town, looking side to side as if she is searching for something she had dropped.

"Leave that one be. She will be no trouble." The Captain says after a moment of silence.

"As you wish."

"Arthur, you have been the most loyal knight within my entire platoon, brigade even. I am appointing you as field commander of the Fourth

Edict. When we return to the kingdom, I believe it is time for you to lead a brigade all on your own.

"Thank you, Captain. I would very much like that. I would give my children something to be proud of."

"I'm sure they are already proud, my friend. When we return, we will return more than soldiers, instead we will be heroes." The Captain removes his helmet and smiles at Arthur. "When your squad is thoroughly ransacked this town, come to me once again. I will have you all guard the prisoner while I prepare for this afternoon.

"As you wish, Captain."

Arthur stands, honoring his captain with a salute before turning and reuniting with his squad.

"Kristoff."

"Yes, Arthur." Kristoff stands and turns to Arthur with a steady posture fit for a leader.

"The Captain wishes for us to return to guard the prisoner at the gallows."

"Very well, did you round up all of the elven women?"

"Yes, except for one. The captain told me to not worry about that one."

"I see, that's odd."

"I thought the same thing, but I will not defy the commands of our leader."

"Very well. Let us return then gentlemen, I'd rather not keep our valiant leader waiting."

Estelle creeps through town, acting as if she has no regard for the Knights who are destroying the town, she calls home. Suddenly she is stopped by Yovanna, whom she has not seen in nearly a week.

"Estelle! Where have you been, I have been looking all over for you. Knights are destroying the town." She says with a trouble look and quivering tone.

"I have been tied up with some errands, I'm sorry."

"It is okay, I'm glad you're safe. Where is your armored idiot at?"

"I do not know. He is off on another contract; I was trying to find out where he would have gone. He promised to take me along."

"Oh, well have you asked the guild master, I'm sure he would help you out."

"Actually, the knights have taken him into custody for helping a criminal of some sort."

"Oh dear, that is not good. Where are they keeping him?"

"One of the knights said they are holding a public trial in the town square, but I have not paid much attention to it."

"Come on, let us go check it out. Maybe we can slip past his guards and talk to him."

"Oh, that is a good idea. Okay." Estelle says cheerfully with a smile. Yovanna takes her hand and begins to jog through the snow filled, yet empty streets.

"Where is everyone?" Yovanna asks curiously, slowing down for a moment.

"I saw a few knights ransacking the town, probably looking for something. Everyone is probably held up in their homes."

"I wonder what this is all about, usually the only knights we see around here are from Vorchid. These men are not from there, their armor is a different color and they seem to be more… official and terrifying."

"They are from Triveria."

"How do you know that?"

"Oh, I've just... seen their symbol in a few books. That is all."

"Oh, I should probably read more, huh." Yovanna chuckles before picking her pace back up.

The two women run into the middle of town, where all the townsfolk have gathered around the gallows built by the knights. Johnathan is sitting with his hands tied behind the gallows, with two members of the Fourth Edict guarding him. The townsfolk have congregated in the front of the gallows where the other two members of the Fourth Edict are standing valiantly like statues made from granite.

"Estelle, look. There is the guild master. Why is he tied up like that, it is supposed to be a trial, and why are there gallows built!?"

"This does not look good; we need to hurry. Can you distract the guards, I will try to sneak over there and talk to Johnathan?"

"I will do my best." Yovanna says with an upbeat tone and determined look on her face.

"Excuse me! Would you two mind helping a poor girl out?" Yovanna asks the two members of the Fourth Edict guarding the rear of the gallows, but they do not budge nor pay her any attention.

"Arthur. Bring that girl to me, you come along too Mattaeus."

"Yes, Captain. Come this way young lady." Arthur answers in a deep, stern voice before taking her arm and guiding her towards the building the Captain is standing by and walking inside with her.

"Now is my chance." Estelle says, crouching and hurrying towards Johnathan who is still unconscious from earlier. "Johnathan" Estelle says, poking him in the face. "Johnathan!" Estelle says a little louder, shaking him awake.

"Estelle, get out of here! It is not safe. Your friend would never forgive me if something were to happen to you."

"Okay, I do not know how much time Yovanna bought me. Two things. Where did Lupin… I mean Levi go. I found his notebook and I know that is his real name."

"Dear heavens. He is never going to forgive me. I sent him to Vorchid to find my sister, she is the leader of Vorchid. Bella Ryker. He should be there by now."

"Okay, that works. Why are you tied up like this, this is not how a trial works?"

"Listen Estelle, you need to find Levi. He is the world's only chance to stop this corruption. They are after him for some reason, they have marked him as a criminal and are destroying town to town trying to find him. I heard a few knights talking about him while in and out of consciousness. Please, find him and stop this madness. I fear I will not be able to greet him again, but when you find him, tell him that Captain Ankore is the reason for…"

"Come on Estelle, let us go. We have to hurry!" Yovanna yells, pulling Estelle away while running towards the outskirts of town.

"Wait Yovanna!"

"There's no time! We have to go, now!"

Yovanna and Estelle run as fast as they can through the thick snow on the ground towards the outskirts of town, trying to escape the sights of all the knights and townsfolk. Estelle looks back for a moment at Johnathan, but in that split-second Arthur's boot collides with his head, knocking him unconscious once again. Blood from the impact pools on the snow-covered ground where he lay unconscious.

"Kristoff, Jameson."

"Yes, Captain." They both answer obediently.

"Follow those two women, they know where the criminal is. That blonde woman was a ruse to catch us off guard. Follow them closely and return with the criminal. We will hold the trial in your absence, so I am keeping Arthur and Matteus here to help."

"Yes, Captain."

The two members of the Fourth Edict saddle their horses and begin a slow trot down the dirt road, tailing Estelle and Yovanna as they ride off into the field on Levi's horse that was left hitched outside of Drixyl.

The short hours that the sun serenades the soft winter air bring a subtle peace throughout the streets of Vorchid. Normally the winter air would deter the merchants and the common rabble from wandering the streets, but they are as vibrant and full of energy today as a summer's day. Levi looks through a window on the ground floor of Maria's home, watching carefully for any danger that might lurk within the busy streets.

"Maria, have you seen any of the Triverian come this way?"

"No, I have not. Why, is there something you are not telling me? It was a little suspicious seeing you pass out at the front gates this morning?" She says, looking up from her book and taking off her glasses.

"I'm just curious. Listen, when the sun sets, I need to find someone named Isabella Ryker. A friend told me to find her."

"Bella? She is the town's Lord. Who told you to find her?"

"I believe her brother, Johnathan, is the guild master in Drixyl."

"Oh, very well. We can go see her after I prepare dinner, does that work?" Maria stands and comes closer to Levi, peeking over his shoulder while his eyes stay locked on the streets.

"That would be fine."

"Now, tell me why you're all the way down here in the sticks. Or do I have to use my magic on you."

"I told you, I'm under orders of the King to clear the countryside of all monster infestations."

"Uh huh. Well, that would be believable, if the Sixth Edict were not already a thing. You are not wearing their armor, nor bear any of the marks of the Triverian army. Your hair is shaggy, and you grew a beard. I'm not an idiot, so tell me why you're here." Maria runs her hands through Levi's untamed hair.

"I'm just following orders."

"Very well. Come. Sit in the chair over there while I start dinner. I'm getting the scissors and you're getting a haircut."

"I'd prefer if you didn't."

"You have no say, I used to cut your hair all the time when we were in our teens."

"Fine." He grumbles as he stands and moves to the wooden chair Maria has placed in the center of the room.

Maria combs Levi's wild hair as a pot of stew is boiling across an open flame flickering on the stovetop. Levi tries to hide his enjoyment with a face of stone, but the soft touch of Maria's hands on his head soothes him more than he could have ever imagined, taking him back to a time when his life was simple and carefree.

"Okay, remember this, I have a blade two inches from your throat, answer wisely. Why are you down here?"

"I told you already."

"Hmm." Maria scoffs as she presses the blade on Levi's neck.

"Listen, Maria. I don't want you to get involved, I just need to find Isabella and then I'll be on my way."

"Okay, that's a start."

"Ah, alright. If the Triverian army comes, you cannot give any information stating you saw me nor gave me shelter. I was accused of a crime against the Kingdom, I found Prince Markor dead in his study, the princess and Ankore found me in the room with him, but it was as if I was molded into stone when they began asking me questions. I choked up and could not speak at all. I do not know what happened. Kristoff helped me escape my cell and I have been on the run ever since."

"What about Amelia? Did you just leave her there?"

"Amelia…"

"Levi, did something happen to her?"

"They… killed her. They decapitated her right in front of me. I… I was not strong enough to save her. I was helpless as I watched the blade pierce through her neck."

"Levi, I'm sorry. If I'd have known I would have come to help at once."

"It is alright, Maria. I just do not wish anyone else to endure the same fate because of my failures. I cannot live with myself knowing that I was the reason she died."

"You need not worry Levi. I will help you any way I can."

"Thank you. I got too comfortable in Drixyl and they caught up to me finally. If it were not for Johnathan, I would have been caught that instant."

"Levi, I must ask, you were accused of a crime and could not speak to defend yourself, correct?"

"Yes, I don't know what came over me, perhaps the shock of finding the prince caused my silence."

"Maybe…" Maria says with a puzzled look on her face. "Okay, all done." She says, removing the blade from Levi's neck and allowing him to stand.

"Thanks, but please Maria, when the time comes, do whatever you must do to keep yourself safe. Do not worry about my safety."

"Very well, I'll be sure to throw you to the wolves." She says with a smirk and nudges him on the arm. "You know, I am really liking the shaggy rouge hairstyle now that it is combed. Keep it for a little while until I get bored of it." Maria chuckles playing with Levi's hair. "Come on, stew should be done. Let us eat and go see Bella before it's too late."

Levi and Maria take to the streets, which appear to be getting busier as the sun falls over the mountains. The merchants are all peddling their goods, workers are steadily loading and unloading ships docked along the Vorchilla river, and the lower class are tending to their street corners begging and offering cheap services to those of wealthy stature as they pass by.

"Maria, this town seems to be wealthier than most across this region of Senary. Why are there so many lower classes within the city?"

"It has not always been this way; I would say a little over six months ago the market here became significantly worse off. Merchants started demanding more for their goods and paying all these beggars they employed far less than their days' worth. The internal economy within Vorchid became saturated with cheap labor and expensive goods. Many of these people lost their homes due to the increased rent and lower pay as well. Quite honestly, everyone has become so riddled with an uncontrollable greed that it has become unbearable. A single meal will cost you five gold from most shops, and a single gallon of milk will run you one gold. I have been studying the economy to figure things out, but I have not been able to decipher anything."

"Six months ago, you said?"

"Yes, it was all sudden, almost overnight the greediness seemed to spread. Even Bella and her council have become greedier, demanding higher taxes from everyone."

"How have you been able to afford living here?"

"Well, I do survey work for Bella, we have become close friends, and being a member of the Sacred Six surely helps when negotiation terms of service."

"I see you have not lost your attitude when it comes to being one of the Kingdoms six."

"Of course not, why would I when I can use it for everything, I've chased my entire life."

"Have it your way. How much farther until we reach Isabella's office."

"Oh, we're not going to her office. Her council can be a bunch of incorrigible asses. We're going to her home, it is right around the corner here."

Maria and Levi quickly push through the crowded streets that are becoming busier through the late afternoon. The air has chilled off now that the sun has started its descent, yet many of the townsfolk are without any sort of warmth in the streets. The moment they turn the corner, Levi is shocked to see the immaculate estate that sits alone overlooking the river just outside of Vorchid. Seven men are working at a steady pace to increase the size of the already immaculate homestead while a middle-aged woman stands on the street supervising their work.

"There she is. Bella, I have brought someone to meet you!" Maria calls out the woman dressed in clean, formal clothing from top to bottom, even her hair tie is seemingly lined with precious gems that demand the highest wealth to obtain.

"Oh, Maria, my dear. How have you been, it's been a little while."

"Yes, it has, this is my friend, Levi" She says, greeting Bella with a soft friendly hug.

"What is she thinking, why would she just blurt out my name like that!? Ah, I should have told her to avoid that." Levi thinks to himself, shaking his head slowly.

"It's a pleasure to meet you, my name is Isabella Ryker, I am the Lord of Vorchid. What brings you to my city?" Bella says with a smile, extending her arm to shake Levi's hand.

Levi shakes her hand. "Pleasure's all mine, Lord Ryker."

"Oh please, call me Bella."

"My apologies, your brother sent me this way. He told me you could assist me in some way or another."

"My brother? What is he trying to do, whore me out again? That son of a bitch."

"No, no. Nothing like that."

"Oh, then very well. Come inside, let us talk." She says, guiding the two inside of her immaculate homestead that bears the same extensiveness of wealth on this inside as it does on the outside. The walls are covered in gorgeous artwork, and every room has an abundance of greenery from all different regions of Senary. "Please, have a seat. Make yourself at home."

"Thank you." Levi says sitting carefully on the luxurious furniture next to Bella.

"You're more than welcome to take your helmet off, I'm sure that thing is heavy."

"I'd prefer to keep it on for the time being, our conversation may be short."

"Oh, very well. What can I do for you?"

"Your brother sent me this way to help me get as far away from this part of Senary as I can."

"And why is that?"

"Ah, I don't want to keep going through this conversation. Why can't people just get to the point." He thinks to himself.

"He's being accused of a crime from the Kingdom, and he needs help to prove his innocence."

"Maria!?"

"You can't just keep running forever. How long before they finally catch up to you?"

"Oh, I see. My brother sent you the right way then. What crime are you being accused of, if I may ask?"

Levi turns his head to Bella. "Murdering the prince, adultery, theft, and treason against the Kingdom."

Isabella moves her head backwards in surprise. "Oh. Dear. Lord."

"Pardon me."

"I'm sorry, that caught me off guard. Normally when someone is on the run from the Kingdom it's over debt or theft, this is... a little more than I expected."

"I understand if you cannot help me, this is something I'm prepared to handle myself, but I need some way to get far away from here."

"Well, if I must say, Maria is right. Running will do you no good. If they've chased you this far, they'll keep chasing you to the ends of Senary and beyond. I believe I can help though; I have some connections in the Kingdom that might be able to assist you."

"Seriously?"

"Yes, but first..."

"Here we go." He thinks to himself. *"I'm going to have to slay a fucking wyvern, I know it."*

Isabella leans forward and looks into Levi's eyes behind his helmet. "Tell me exactly who you are."

Levi sits back in his seat and takes a deep breath. "My name is Levi Timeré, I am known within the Kingdom as the Wolf. I bear the Mark of the Wolf and I am a chosen member of the Sacred Six."

"Oh, how prestigious. So, I assume being a member of the chosen, you can wield a sword?"

"Yes."

"Good. Well, I require a favor in return for my help. I require you to travel to Kreitor, I have received reports from guards that there are numerous monster attacks and murders happening there. We used to supply goods to the people of Kreitor, but since the attacks, I have put an end to this. They were a very good supplier of precious material due to their abundant forest surrounding the village until about six months ago ."

"Okay, I can handle that."

"Take Maria with you." She says as she spreads a map across the finely crafted wooden table in the center of them. "Do you see these hexagonal structures here across Senary. There are six evenly aligned across our northern region here, and a seventh, smaller structure in the center of Triveria."

"Yes, I have noticed them before. I assumed they were some sort of religious monument."

"Well, in history, each one bears a mark of one of the chosen. Each one specifically matched to a mark. This one here, directly above Kreitor, bears the Mark of the Ox, I believe it may have something to do with the monster attacks, but I have no information because no one has come back alive if they have gotten close. As a chosen Six, you may be able to. Go there, kill the monsters, record what you

find, and report back to me. I will get into contact
with my friends in the Kingdom and try to help you
out."

"I can do that; I will leave at once."

"My, you are a go getter. Be careful, the
monsters that have been sighted there are not
normal for the region."

"Maria, are you coming?" Levi says as he
stands and walks towards the door.

"Yes, the faster we leave the faster we can get
back and I can return to my books."

"It was nice meeting you Levi, and Maria,
take care of him. He may be more important to this
world than you think." Bella says with a smile as
she returns to studying her map.

"Okay Levi, let us return to my house and
get supplies and we will leave at once."

"Okay, lead the way." Levi says in agreeance, as they quickly make their way through the crowded streets towards Maria's home.

As the sun sets on the streets of Drixyl, all the townsfolk gather around the freshly assembled gallows in the town square. Johnathan is the center of attention, standing with his hands and feet tied together, and a noose around his neck. Captain Ankore makes his way up the steps, dressed in full armor and a sword sheathed at his side. The townsfolk all chatter quietly as the two members of the Fourth Edict stand guard at the base of the gallows, glaring at the crowd.

"Attention fine people of Drixyl. I am Captain Theodore Ankore, I am the leader of this platoon of soldiers you see around your humble town. We have come in search of a criminal to the Kingdom. I am sure you have seen our posters hanging around town and you have all graciously answered our questions willingly. I thank you for that. This man, your guild master, Johnathan Ryker, is accused of helping the criminal by alerting him of our arrival in your town, allowing him time to escape." Captain Ankore says sternly, looking out towards the crowd, the whispers slowly fade throughout the crowd as their attention has all turned towards Johnathan, with a disturbed look of disbelief on their faces. "I deemed it best to hold a public trial for this accomplice, mind you, the criminal we are after is found guilty for murdering the first born son of the King, Prince Markor Triveria the third, raping the Second born, the Princess Raina Triveria the second, stealing precious gems, information, and gold from the King's chambers, and committing acts of treason against the King while he stood trial. What say you for this man standing before me?" He asks sternly, as the crowd still falls silent, most just watch with a look of anger painted upon their face. "We have written evidence signed by Johnathan Ryker, a letter he gave to Levi Timeré, the criminal, warning him of our arrival. Do you, the fine people of this town, find this man innocent." Captain Ankore says, removing his helmet and scanning the crowd with a vicious bloodthirsty scowl. "Or, GUILTY!?"

"Guilty." The crowd all murmurs sporadically.

"You have decided the fate of this criminal. Thank you for your cooperation."

Captain Ankore places his helmet upon his head once again and looks to Johnathan who is hanging his head down, tears soaking through the wrap upon his eyes.

"Be warned humble people of this town. This is the fate of those who defy the will of the King." Captain Ankore says sternly.

The Captain draws his sword and with all the strength he can muster, he drives the sword into the rope holding the trapdoor below Johnathan's feet. The sword sticks nearly four inches into the rough-cut wood the gallows were built from, and Johnathan falls through the floor. In a split second, Johnathan reaches the end of the rope holding the noose around his neck, with a quick jerk from the weight of his body falling on the rope. His neck snaps, sending a shutter down everyone who witnesses' spine, a sound that all who saw will remember for their entire lives. A feeling of fear, sorrow, and anger overwhelm the people of the town, as Johnathan's lifeless body hangs from the gallows, slowly swaying from side to side.

Chapter 5: Windows in the Shadow

Through the setting sun peeking through the trees, Levi and Maria trot down the snow struck path eastbound towards the village of Kreitor. With the night air creeping in slowly, the cold begins to take a toll on Maria. Upon their horse, Levi feels her begin to shiver.

"Getting cold?"

"No, no. I'm fine."

"Right, your lips are turning blue."

"What?! No, they're not!" She says, feeling the warmth of her own breath on her lips.

"Take my cloak." Levi says, pulling off the thick black cloak from his shoulders and wrapping it around Maria instead.

"Thank you, but what about you? How will you stay warm?"

"I'll be fine, it is not my first time in the wilderness amidst the winter air."

"Have it your way. Kreitor is not much farther, just another mile or so. Do you think it is best to set up camp in the village?" She says with a look hinting towards a hidden intent behind her kind eyes.

"Most likely not, if there have been frequent monster attacks then we will have no choice but to return to Vorchid directly after we tend to the matter here."

"Oh, very well..." Maria utters a disheartened tone.

"Maria, keep your head forward, do not look away from the road. Understand?"

"Why?"

"Other travelers. I cannot see them clearly yet; they may be a part of the Triverian platoon from Drixyl."

"No need to worry, you have got a helmet on and I am still held in high regard within Triveria."

Levi keeps his gaze steady towards the path ahead of them, trying to get a glimpse of the travelers from his peripheral vision, though his helmet is making the task quite difficult. Suddenly he hears a woman's voice call out to him in the distance, then again as the travelers come closer and closer.

"Maria, stay here." Levi says as he steps down from his horse and places his hand on the hilt of his sword sheathed across his back, ready to draw at any moment. On the hilt of his sword, the acidic saliva from the basilisk has eaten through the cross guards as well as the moleskin glove under his gauntlet. Maria watches closely as Levi readies himself for his moment to strike.

"Levi!" The young woman's voice chimes again through his ears.

Levi throws his head back in discontent. "God damnit. Estelle!"

"Levi, do you know them?" Maria asks, wrapped in Levi's cloak.

"I know one of them it seems. She is a pain in the ass." He says removing his hand from his hilt and fixing his gauntlet that has slipped down his hand a little farther because of the missing moleskin underneath.

Estelle and Yovanna trot up to Levi and Maria through the thick snow. Before their horse can even come to a stop, Estelle slides off the back of the horse and runs over to Levi, punching his armor-plated chest with all the strength she can muster.

"Ouch!" Estelle wails, shaking her hand in pain. "I should seriously kick your ass right now. What the hell is wrong with you? Seriously? Treating me well, keeping me safe, telling me to go home, lying to me, and just running away!? I would have come with you! I've never met such an insufferable person to be around and I cannot stand you!" Estelle yells at Levi, tears welling in her eyes and her face becoming beat red with anger.

Levi looks down at her through the small openings in his damaged helmet's eye holes. "Are you done?"

"Oh, do not even speak to me! I will seriously kick your ass right now!" She yells once again, crossing her arms with a heavy aura of anger and frustration overwhelming her. She looks towards Levi with her beautiful amethyst eyes shimmering in the setting sun, wooing Levi through the holes in his helmet. "What? Just going to stand there and look at me like the idiot you are? Say something, jackass!"

"You told me not to speak to you."

"I was frustrated! I still am! Ugh." She scoffs, now pouting as her tears of anger dry in the cold winter air.

"Um, excuse me. Mr. Levi, Estelle, it is cold. Can we go now?" Yovanna asks with an innocent tone, wrapping her cloak around herself.

"Ah, yes. I am sorry Yovanna I just could not hold it in any longer. I needed to yell at him."

A thunderous trot of two horses quickly approached from the south where Estelle and Yovanna came from, rushing towards the quartet of people standing in the cold winter air. Levi takes Estelle's arm and moves her behind him quickly once again placing his hand upon his swords hilt and reading himself for battle. Estelle notices Levi's gauntlet has been almost eaten by something, along with the cross guards on his sword.

"Stay behind me, Estelle." Levi says sternly.

"I can handle myself!" Estelle says with an angry tone as Levi stands in front of her.

Two men from the Fourth Edict leap from their horses, drawing their swords as they land and steadily approach the group.

"We have no quarrel with any of you, leave us be." Levi says, preparing to draw his sword and strike.

"Sir, remove your helmet and lay down your sword at this very moment." Jameson says with a grandiose tone.

"I refuse."

Jameson steps back into a battle stance, readying himself for a lunge. "So be it, Levi Timeré."

Just before he can make the first strike towards Levi, Kristoff sinks his sword deep into the opening between Jameson's helmet and breastplate. Kristoff wraps his arm around Jameson's chest as the blood from his neck seeps out like a culvert.

"I am terribly sorry, Jameson. You were a good Soldier."

"Kristoff… why would you betray me… we were like brothers."

"We were nothing more than soldiers in the same squad. Rest easy, soldier." Kristoff says, lowering Jameson to the ground and removing his knife from Jameson's throat. Kristoff removes his helmet and drops it in the deep snow next to him.

His ears twitch with excitement as he walks towards Levi. "It has been too long, my friend."

"Kristoff…" Levi drops his guard and embraces his long-lost friend with a hug, the clang of their metal breastplates rings through the valley like two blades meeting each other perfectly.

"Looks like I am a criminal now too, could not let you have all the fun, now could I?" He chuckles as he releases his grip from his friend.

"Kristoff, you should have stayed in the Kingdom. You have done more than enough to help me this far."

"We are even now; you have saved my life twice. I saved you in Triveria, count this as the second. Listen, your brother has gone mad with power in Drixyl."

"What do you mean?"

"Theodore has lost his mind, he forged a note stating the guild master was guilty of helping you and held a public trial this afternoon. He executed him in front of the entire town."

Levi shakes his head in disbelief. "Dear Lord. Johnathan… This is my fault; I should have stayed. He would not have met his demise like this."

"Excuse me, who are you again?" Estelle asks the black and white Lynx man standing in front of Levi.

"Oh, pardon my manners. My name is Kristoff Crowson, Levi and I grew up together. We are much like brothers, and who might you three be… wait a second. Maria!?"

Maria shakes her head. "Good evening, Kristoff. It has been awhile."

"Yes! Yes, it has, how have you been!? Come here give me a hug!" Kristoff joyfully yells, approaching Maria.

"I will have to ask you to wait for our reuniting celebration. You are covered in blood, and these are new clothes."

"Oh my, you have not changed at all. Still as posh and stuck up as ever."

"You watch your tone, when you can beat me in a battle of wits then you can dishonor me any way you wish." Maria says with her nose pointed towards the sky.

"Oh, bullocks. You have the wits of a spring hen."

"Enough you two. We have a task to complete."

"Excuse me!" Estelle pushes in front of Levi and faces Kristoff. "My name is Estelle Fellistar, this is Yovanna Marietta."

"Pleasure to meet you." Yovanna says with a soft blush and kind smile.

Kristoff bows formally to the two women. "The pleasure is all mine."

"Pardon me, little girl. Estelle was it? You said your last name is Fellistar, as in the elven kingdom in the southeast, Fellistar?" Maria asks inquisitively, though Estelle falls silent for a moment.

"I do not retain any sort of relation with my family. I am just a traveler, and I am a grown woman. I kindly ask you to refer to me as such."

"I see." Maria says, pulling out her notebook and jotting down a few notes.

"Kristoff, what should we do with the body?"

"Well, it'd be wise to hide it for the time being. I will throw him on my horse and stash him somewhere far away from here. Where were you heading by the way?"

"We are heading to Kreitor to take care of a monster infestation for Isabella Ryker in Vorchid. She is going to help me out, but I needed to scratch her back first."

"Ryker, as in relation to Johnathan Ryker in Drixyl?"

"Yes… that's his sister. I do not believe she will take it well that her brother was executed by the Triverian army."

"No, no she will not. But that is a problem for us in the future. Come on, let us go fight some monsters. I am all feisty after that little interaction."

Levi nods to Kristoff. "Very well, let us go."

The group saddles their horses. Estelle insists on riding with Levi, while the others can have their own horse. Levi does not pay much mind to it, though Maria glances at them from time to time, noticing that Estelle is clutching Levi's waist tightly with her face placed over his shoulder. She scoffs and continues following Levi's path through the snow along with the others.

Their short ride to Kreitor was filled with reminiscing over good time between the three childhood friends, though mostly Kristoff and Levi chatting of their adventures as teenagers. Estelle and Yovanna listened patiently, giggling along to their blunders and missteps through their years together. The pleasant feeling of friends reuniting wards of the feelings of depravity Levi has been suffering from for a long time, under his helmet a small smile peeks through; giving Levi a feeling that he had long forgotten since his time in the Kingdom of Triviera. Levi wished this feeling would last forever and a day, although a pressure suddenly began to weigh on the delighted spirits of the group. As if an aura of calamity suddenly surrounded them like smoke from a house fire. The horses began to wine and buck as they approached the foothill village, as if something is scaring them severely. Levi and Kristoff tried to calm their steeds, but to no avail the horses wished to run, far, far away from this place. The group dismounts their horses and stands just outside of the village for a moment, glaring into the bustling town full of life. A few merchants are peddling goods, while children play in the street. The homes are all well-kept, not a single sign of rot meets their eyes from a distance. Levi turns to Kristoff and shrugs before taking a step into the village.

Suddenly the pleasant views are faded into dust as if it were just an illusion, the homes are destroyed, some burnt to the ground. Deformed humanoid creatures are running back and forth through the village, feeding on something reeking of rotting flesh. The humanoid creatures notice Levi and Kristoff standing at the entrance, staring as if they are caught in a trance, before running into the broken homesteads to hide.

"Kristoff, what in the world is going on here?"

"Some sort of black magic, this is unruly, disgusting even. That stench, heavens above that stench." He says covering his nose to hide from the smell.

Levi draws his blade, realizing how deteriorated it has become from the basilisk's saliva. He lets out a sigh and walks forward into the village a little farther. A black fog begins to roll down from the hill where the structure of the Ox is said to lay. Before Levi can comprehend the situation, a barrage of footsteps and hisses ring in his ears as six of the creatures lunge towards him. Kristoff rushes to his aid with his blade drawn, together they slash and strike the beasts attacking them. In a split second, more of the creatures appear from the homesteads and advance on the two warriors.

"Kristoff, what have we gotten ourselves into?" Levi says, back to back with Kristoff as the creatures attack them from every direction. Slicing through their flesh as if it were a rotting corpse.

"I have no idea, my friend. This is going to get out of hand quickly."

"Levi, what are you doing?" Estelle asks inquisitively, who is standing just a few feet from him.

"Get out of the village! It is not safe!" Levi yells to Estelle.

"What has gotten into you, there is nothing here? Just burnt down homes and corpses."

"What!?" Levi asks in a fit. Suddenly Levi is pulled by the shoulder onto the ground dragged through the thick black fog that has engulfed him entirely. Losing consciousness immediately.

"Where am I?" Levi asks himself; he asks himself while standing in a void it seems. Entirely dark except for an array flickering torches surrounding him. "Am... am I dead?"

"Levi, my son."

"Father!?" Levi yells into the void.

"Levi, can you hear me?"

Levi turns around and removes his helmet. "Yes father, I can hear you! Where are you!?"

"Right here, son." Levi turns around rapidly to see his father standing before him. His father is a spitting image of him, though his hair has a pearly white tint to it and his beard is trimmed into a neat goatee.

"Father..." Levi hugs his father endearingly as tears well in his eyes.

"Son, I have been watching your path. You have been through a lot, and I am sorry I have not been able to help you." Levi's father says holding

Levi's shoulders, looking at him with a sincere disappointment in his eyes for himself.

"Father, it is not your fault. You've given me everything I could have ever asked for, everything you have ever taught me has kept me going this entire time."

"Levi perhaps it is time you learn the truth of my death. Walk with me."

Levi's father turns and walks towards one of the torches in the void, where the orange flame changes to a steady blue glow. The void augments into a window, looking through his eyes in the last moments of his life. The King is standing directly in front of him, with a scowl that could pierce the soul of the Devil.

"Is that, the King?"

"Yes, he was the one that took my life."

"The King!? That bastard!"

"Calm down Levi, just watch closely."

Levi watches closely through the window of his father's soul and watches the King stare intently at him, as if he were living his father's last moments.

"William, you dare to defy me?"

"Your highness, he is my son. He would never do such terrible things; I do not care what some legend says. I raised him as a proper man, not a murderer!"

"William, it is not a matter of how he was raised. There is a demon within that boy, I want him executed at once! Bring him to me!"

"I refuse."

"William! That demon will bring ruin to my entire Kingdom, the very thing my family has built through centuries of conquest and determination! I will not let some worthless man and the Devil destroy it!"

"He is not the Devil! He is my son! Give him a chance to prove himself!"

"Why? Why should I give the Devil a chance in my Kingdom!?"

"Because he is not the Devil of the legend!"

"He was born with the Mark of the Wolf! The legend foretells the destruction he will bring!"

"You have no right to murder my son over some legend that you yourself have no idea if it is even real! What proof do you have!?"

"The council has demanded I take action; these men and women have lived through the calamity of the Wolf time and time again! I will believe their words more than yours!"

A silence breaks the conversation, tears begin to well in William's eyes and his eyes look towards the stone floor of the King's throne room.

"Your highness, if you so believe that my son is the Devil, then what does that make me, the father of the Devil!?"

"You are just a man; you have nothing to do with this!"

"Markor! What is all this fuss about!?" A woman in an elegant dress says.

"My lady. Please forgive me. I am just talking with William over the boy with the Mark of the Wolf."

"He is your son, is he not, William?"

"Yes, your majesty." He says, drying his eyes with his hand.

"Markor, what do you intend to do with the boy?"

"I will have him executed, promptly."

"I will not allow this; a boy can cause no harm to this Kingdom."

"You have no say in this. This is for the good of the Kingdom!"

"Markor, I am your wife. I have equal say for the good of the Kingdom."

"Shut up!" The King yells at his wife, striking her in the face, causing her to fall onto the stone floor.

"My Queen!" William yells, dropping to his knees to check on the Queen, touching the cut on her face from the King's rings.

"Do not touch her!" The King yells, kicking William from his knees onto the ground.

"How dare you hurt the woman you say you love! What kind of man are you, what kind of King!"

"If you will not give me the boy, I will have to take him by force!"

"I will not let you!" William yells standing, ready to brawl with the King.

In the blink of an eye, William feels a knife pierce through his gut. He looks down and his body is struck with shock for a moment. He steps back looking at the King.

"I… I will not let you. I will protect my son!" William yells, pulling the knife from his gut and struggles to escape from the King.

"You will die!" The King yells, plunging a sword through William's chest.

William falls to the ground, coughing up blood as his life fades along with his consciousness.

"My… son…"

"Do not fret, William. You will be reunited with your son very soon."

Levi's mind is overcome with anger, a rage like a volcano that's been dormant for a millennium, ready to explode at a moment's notice.

"I will kill the bastard!" Levi yells as a black aura appears around him, absorbing the darkness from the void into his body.

"It seems your time has come my son, someday, we will meet again." William says with a smile on his face as he looks at his son.

"What!? Father, what do you mean?"

"It is not your time. Wake up Levi."

Levi suddenly jolts awake in a fit of rage, he flails his arms, snapping back to what he thought was reality. Kristoff, Estelle, Maria, and Yovanna are all standing at his side.

"Levi! You are alive!" Estelle yells with a joyful smile on her face.

"Where am I, what happened?"

"We are just outside of Kreitor now, are you feeling alright?" Kristoff asks.

"I'm fine, what happened?" Levi asks again, becoming frustrated again.

"You and I walked into Kreitor and everything just... changed. The houses were destroyed, and corpses lie everywhere in the streets. After a few steps in you started, hallucinating. Swinging your sword at creatures but nothing was there. I backed away thankfully, or else you would have cut my damn head off."

"How did I end up here?"

"A black fog rolled down from the hill and you blacked out as soon as it engulfed you. I was able to pull you out of Kreitor, but I almost met the same fate."

"I remember the fog, but you are telling me that the human-like monsters weren't even real?"

"No, there was nothing there."

"Did anyone get hurt?"

"No, you were the only one who breathed in the black fog. You said you were going to Kreitor to fight monsters, did Isabella say what kind of monsters there were?"

"She only said there were unusual reports, ones not found in this region."

"Perhaps those who witnessed these unusual monsters succumb to the same thing you did."

"I am going back in, I need answers."

"Like hell you are, I pulled you out of there once. Do you think I am going to do it again? Absolutely not, you will die in there and I will laugh in your lifeless face"

"I am sure I will be fine. I have an idea."

"Levi, stop. We cannot return there without research." Maria pulls Levi's arm trying to stop him from entering the village again.

"Call it research then." Levi jerks his arm free from Maria's grip and walks into the village once again, scanning the area for any differences between his last experience.

"Levi! Stop it!" Estelle yells out, running into the village with Levi. She grabs Levi's shoulder and halts his movement.

"Estelle, do you see anything?"

"There's just corpses."

"Look closer." Estelle takes a moment and scans the village once again, looking closely at the dead bodies and the homes.

"The people look like they have caught the disease, they were not killed by monsters. And the homes are... rotten. The wood has turned black for some reason. Do you think it is because of the fog?"

"I do not know. Here, tie this under your nose and keep close to me." He says, handing her a piece of charcoal.

"Charcoal?"

"It can be used as a filter, breathe only through your nose and do not talk. Just stay close." He says sternly, tucking a piece of charcoal under his helmet.

Levi and Estelle walk side by side through the black fog that is rolling down from the hill above Kreitor. Examining the homesteads and corpses as they slowly walk past. Estelle tugs on Levi's arm and points towards one of the homesteads, then to her ear. Levi turns and moves Estelle behind him. He draws his sword and walks slowly towards the homestead. Levi listens closely, and through the soft whisper of the wind through the trees, a faint cry is heard from inside one of the homes. He takes a step into the homestead and the floorboards crack instantly as if they have been rotten for a century. The crying inside the homestead is a little louder and has turned into a soft whimper as if it is being muffled. Levi steps through carefully peeking around each corner. The black fog has entirely engulfed the home making it extremely difficult to see in the near pitch-black home. He pulls a lantern from a hook on the wall and lights it. The dim light emanating from the lantern gives off just enough light to see in front of them. In the shadowy fog a deteriorated metal handle casts a shadow on the floor from the flickering lantern. Levi turns his head to Estelle and gestures towards the cellar door. He creaks it open and the hinges snap as it reaches its peak. Levi drops the remainder of the door on the floor and steps down the stone cellar stairs. The small cellar is clear of the black fog and the flickering lantern reveals a small girl, maybe seven or eight years old, huddled in the corner. Whimpering, malnourished, and crying. Levi approaches her slowly as Estelle climbs down the stairs. He sets the lantern on the ground and crouches in front of the girl.

"Are you alright?"

The frightened young girl is in shock over something, cold and shivering with a canvas sack wrapped around her. Levi removes his cloak and wraps it around the young girl. He takes another piece of charcoal from his pouch and ties it around her nose and lifts her into his arms.

"Estelle, grab the lantern."

"Okay, is she alright?"

"I think she will be okay, she is just frightened." Estelle watches as Levi holds the young girl closely as a father would a daughter. She smiles as he carries her up the stairs and follows him closely. Levi stands atop the stairs waiting for the lantern's guiding light. He nods his head forward towards the open door to the home, gesturing Estelle to lead the way out. Following closely, Levi holds the young girl tight in his arms covering him from the winter air as they emerge from the home and into the streets, covering her eyes from the unruly sight of corpses lying on the ground. Estelle guides their path out of the black fog back onto the snowy path where the group is waiting nervously for their counterparts.

"Estelle!" Yovanna yells excitedly, leaping towards Estelle and hugging her. Tears well in her eyes. "I was so worried about you! Are you okay!? What happened!?" Levi emerges from the black fog holding the young girl in his arms, her crying has stopped though her shivering has not.

"Maria, take this girl and go back to Vorchid. I found her in one of the homes, she is malnourished and freezing. Get her to a doctor as soon as you can. Same with the rest of you, go back with them. I will be back later in the evening."

"I am not going anywhere; I am staying with you." Estelle says approaching Levi with determination in her voice.

"You are a pain sometimes, you know that?"

"Good, now you know how it feels."

"Levi, what happened in there?" Maria asks curiously.

"A black fog is rolling down from the hill, the homes are all deteriorated and crumbling. Everyone in the village is dead it seems, besides that girl. I am going back in and checking out where the fog is coming from. Oh, and Kristoff, I'm counting this as a time you were wrong."

"What!? I wasn't wrong about anything!"

"You swore I would die in there, but here I am." Levi chuckles as his friend wells with anger.

"Levi take these vials, get some samples of the fog for me. I'll do some tests on them, find out what they are." Maria says handing Levi four small glass vials with metal caps.

"Oh, look at you, Ms. science woman with her glass jars. Just use your fancy magic and collect some samples." Kristoff half scoffs, half chuckles. Maria slaps him on the rear of his head, startling him. "Hey!"

"Come on now, we need to hurry back to Vorchid."

"Kristoff, do you have any charcoal on you."

"Oh, yes. They are in my pouch here." Levi takes four more pieces of charcoal from Kristoff's pouch and hands two to Estelle. "Oh, I see. You took a trick out of your father's book I see."

"It seemed to work, but I am afraid the charcoal is not going to be very effective for long based on the way the homes are deteriorated."

"Right, have fun you two. Do not stay out too late, dinner will be on the table when you get home." Kristoff says chuckling as he mounts his horse with the young girl in front of him. Estelle blushes and looks towards the ground trying not to laugh.

"Stay safe Estelle, I want to hear all about this when you get back!" Yovanna says, jumping on her horse as well.

The group rides off down the snow-covered path towards Vorchid as the sun finally sets across the white glistening valley outside of Kreitor.

"Are you ready Estelle? Make sure you replace the charcoal first."

"I am ready. What's your plan?" She asks with an excited smile.

"I want to find out about this fog, something just doesn't feel right about it. We're going to follow it up the hill towards the source and see if we can find anything out."

"Okay, wonderful. Let us go."

"Remember this charcoal probably will not last long, we will use one piece on the walk up and change it out once we reach the top."

Estelle nods in agreeance as the two enter the black fog engulfing only the town of Kreitor. Their stride is a bit deeper this time as they feel confident in the charcoal's ability to protect them from the dangerous clouds surrounding them. Making their way up the hill, Levi notices the trees have lost their limbs, the soft wind is cracking and breaking branches from the top of the tall leafless trees and falling to the ground. The entire forest is seemingly dead, even the young trees barely thicker than a man's leg have died as well. Nearing the top of the hill, Levi notices a bright white light shining towards the sky through the fog. He taps Estelle on the shoulder and points before increasing his pace up the hill.

Upon reaching the top, a large stone hexagon is erected a few inches from the ground. Levi is the first to step into the structure, realizing the mark in the center of the structure is emanating the light. He examines it for a moment, turning his head to the side.

"The Mark of the Ox, the same one the Prince had." He thinks to himself.

"Levi, look the fog is not touching the stones up here." Estelle says, removing the charcoal wrapped around her face.

Levi pulls the piece from his helmet and tosses it over the hill into the thick fog. "You're right, how odd."

"What is this place?" Estelle asks.

"It is a shrine of some sort, belonging to one the Sacred Six of Legend. This one bears the Mark of the Ox."

"The Ox? Oh wait! I have read of the Sacred Six, I have a little book right here all about them!" Estelle says pulling a small brown leather backed book from her satchel.

"I did not know there were any books about them."

"This was my mother's book, she used to tell me stories of the Sacred Six. How they are destined to save the world from the end of time." Estelle flips through the book, finding the pages written about the Mark of the Ox.

"Interesting."

"Oh, right here. The Ox is said to bear the weight of the avarice of the world. Thought so, each of the six bares the weight of something different from the world. Why is this one lit though?"

"I'm not sure. It is all rather odd if you ask me. Why is the fog emanating from the outside of the structure? Does your book say anything?"

"Let's see." Estelle flips through the pages, skimming each one rapidly.

"Nope, not a thing about any sort of fog."

"Odd, let us collect these samples and return to Vorchid before night fully sets in. It will be too cold to camp this evening."

"Okay." Estelle flips back through her small book and reads each page while Levi carefully collects samples from the edge of the structure. Estelle's eyes jolt back and forth across each page quickly, but suddenly she stops, and a look of confusion overcomes her expression.

"Ready to go?" Levi asks.

"Yes, do you know anything of the Sacred Six?"

"I know a little, that's about it."

"What does this mean?" She asks, pointing to the page in her book. "He who bears the Mark of the Wolf will decipher the outcome of the stones?"

"I do not know. Seems rather vague to me."

"I wonder if Maria has any more books on the Six, she told me a lot about them while you were unconscious."

"She might, she has always collected books, even as a child." Estelle looks towards Levi with curiosity in her eyes. "Come on, let us head back."

Estelle and Levi prepare themselves for their journey back through the black fog, wrapping the last two pieces of charcoal around their nose and pushing forward through the illusionary wall surrounding the stone structure.

As they continue down the mountain, the dead trees crack even more violently as the wind picks up. Levi is keeping a close watch on their path ahead, making sure the dangerous branches known as widowmakers do not crash down on their heads. Estelle is following behind Levi; the fog is deterring the moon's light from guiding their path. Levi's eyes are adjusted to traveling in the night, although this is as if they are moving through a cavern with only sound to guide their path. Estelle places her hand on Levi's arm, holding tightly so as to not lose him. Levi notices a dim torch in the distance in the village, and then seven more appear, sparking in a specific order it seems. Figures dressed in white appear in front of each torches, Levi sees them clearly through the fog. Levi takes Estelle's hand and pulls her towards him as he increases his pace through the fog. Just before they reach the torches and figures, they all fade as if they were nothing but ash.

"Come on Estelle, we have to hurry!" Levi's steady walk turns to a sprint with Estelle holding his hand right beside him. Through the thick fog they ran, it felt to them as if they were running for an hour even though they were already near the exit of the village. Estelle is the first to burst through the fog, she immediately turns around realizing Levi is not with her yet. She watches closely as the fog that has engulfed her body is almost vacuumed back into the village of Kreitor.

"Le…" She begins to say but is interrupted by Levi leaping through the fog and rolling onto the ground, coughing as if he were gasping for air. "Levi are you okay!?" She asks, falling to her knees next to him. He unstraps his helmet and throws it from his head, sitting up and gasping for air. Estelle feels an overwhelming rush of feelings as she sees his face for the first time.

She blushes and shakes her head. "Levi, talk to me. Are you alright?"

"Yes… I am fine."

"What happened, you did not come out as soon as I did?"

"I ran into something, like a stone wall it felt like. I do not understand what happened." He says coming to a standing position and looking for his helmet. "Are you feeling alright?"

"Yes, I am fine. The charcoal worked fine for me; I did not have any trouble through the fog."

"Did you see the torches?" He asks.

"No, I did not see anything at all. I could barely see you, that is why I grabbed your arm." Levi slides his helmet on and a piece of charcoal falls from the opening in the bottom. The piece is small and deteriorated as if it was eaten. Estelle picks it up and removes the tie from around her nose, comparing the two pieces. Estelle's piece is much larger, approximately three times as big and has barely been weathered at all it seems.

"Come on, let us head back." He says, saddling the last horse standing on the other side of the snow-covered path, he extends his hand to assist Estelle onto the horse. She places the pieces of charcoal in her pouch and takes Levi's hand onto the horse.

The night air brings a bone chilling wind across the valley. The powdery snow blows in every direction creating small whirlwinds in the open flats as they ride swiftly down the path towards Drixyl. Estelle feels Levi's body shake from the cold wind causing him to shiver. She looks closely at his armor, realizing the black fog began to deteriorate the steel plates covering his body. A few pieces have fallen off from the broken leather straps. She looks down at her clothing, but hers are completely fine besides a few of her buckles that have been chewed up a little.

"Are you cold?"

"No, I will be fine."

"Stop the horse for a second." She says Levi pulls the reins and the horse comes to a slow stop.

Estelle ducks under Levi's arm and moves the front of the horse. Pressing tightly against him and removing the cloak from her shoulder. "Wrap this around us, your armor will give you frostbite in this wind." Levi pauses for a moment, then wraps the cloak around the two of them. Estelle takes the ends and pulls them tightly together, pressing against Levi tightly. Levi's helmet hides his facial expression, though the blush on his face sends a warming sensation down his whole body.

"Ready?" He asks hesitantly.

Estelle smiles as she looks towards Levi. "Yep."

Their journey continues through the valley, trotting steadily on their horse. The moon's dim light reflects on the snow allowing them to see the beauty of the valley for what it is. Estelle watches as they pass by each farm and forest, smiling the entire way.

"You know Levi when I left home. I just wanted to run as far away as I could. When I met Yovanna and made my first friend, I felt the worry and anxiety just fade away. It felt like I made the right decision, but it was not until our paths crossed that I found a direction. I cannot explain it, but when I am with you, things just feel... right. I have had a lot of trouble throughout my life, and I ran because something told me to. I never understood what it was, but I feel as if I was meant to run forever until I found you. I have only known you for a few days, and quite honestly, we do not know anything about each other, but I know deep down this is where I am meant to be. Right here with you." She says with the same wonderful smile on her face as Levi saw when he awoke from the void.

"Estelle, it is not safe to be around me."

"I do not mind. What is the point of life if you live safely in hiding?"

"I am not a good man, I have done terrible things, and my journey will force my hand to do more. It is not wise to follow me around like this."

"What is the definition of a good man? Or a bad one at that? You saved my life on the mountain that day, and again on the walk down. Yovanna said you carried me all the way down the mountain making sure I was safe. You did not have to do that, so what about that makes you a bad man, and not a good one?"

"I'm sure you have heard the rumors in Drixyl when the knights arrived. I'm criminalized for murder."

"I do not believe that for a second. I knew you were hiding from the knights; I did not know why though."

"How did you know?"

"You knew what language they were speaking when we were heading to Levenwood, and your insistence to camp and wait for any more of the basilisks in the daylight. Basilisks are nocturnal for one, and they have never traveled in pairs. They live in solitude. I am not an idiot. Also, your moniker was... stupid. Also, I found your notebook."

"You are a pain in the ass, sometimes."

"Well get used to it, because I am not going anywhere." She says with a chuckle.

"Estelle, why did you leave your home.? You bear the name of the Elven kingdom. Clearly you are royalty." Estelle looks down towards the back of the horse and thinks for a moment. The silence creates a feeling of tension in the air. "You do not have to tell me if you wish, it's out of place for me to ask."

"No... no. I will tell you; it just brings up bad memories that's all. My father is the King and my mother the Queen of Fellistar. In the Elven region, the Queen is the ruler of the Kingdom, and the father is always married into the royal family. My mother always raised me and treated me right, she taught me everything I know. But my father was... abusive. He felt as if he was inferior to my mother because she ruled the Kingdom rather than him. My mother loved him dearly still, though he beat me senselessly when I was a child and teenager. Later in the years after I learned how to fight, he stopped abusing me and began abusing my mother. One day I just lost it, I was overcome with anger and sorrow for my mother as she just took the abuse and never said a word. It made me feel sorry for her, and I began to hate her for being helpless. I could not take it any longer, one day I just lost control. The commotion took place in the morning one day and continued until the evening. My mother was being beat mercilessly, all I could hear was her crying, and him yelling at her for being a worthless Queen. I sat in my room day after day listening to it and that day, I just lost myself in my emotions. When the commotion stopped, I heard him snoring and I could hear my mother sobbing in her bedroom. I snuck in... and I killed my father. I sliced his throat and stabbed him in the heart. My mother just watched as I did it. She cried even harder, asking what I had done. She called me a monster, screaming that she loved him, and the abuse was going to stop. He was a good man, and my own father." Levi listened patiently as she told her past story, quietly giving her the time to speak. "I fought the tears back in my own eyes, realizing how deteriorated my mother's mind had become. Then I realized why she never stopped him from abusing me and was perfectly fine with being abused herself. She lost herself in the love she felt for him, and I lost all feelings I had of kindness towards her. I packed a small bag of my things and I ran. I ran for two years, bouncing from town to town before I ended up in Drixyl and met Yovanna, and then you. Sorry for the long story."

"No need to be sorry. Estelle?"

"Yes?"

"I would have done the same thing. I am sorry you had to go through that your entire life."

"It's fine. It made me who I am today."

"Our past defines our present, but the history we create today defined our future. Can I promise you something?"

"Sure, I guess." She says with slight confusion in her voice.

"You'll never have to go through that sort of tragedy again. Even if I were to die, I will make sure you live a good life. I promise."

Tears well slightly in Estelle's eyes as a silence overcame the two. "Do not say that."

"I can assure you that you will have a good life. I have enough friends that will make sure you will be alright."

"Do not say that, Levi. I don't want to hear that!" Estelle says, beginning to cry.

"What?"

"Don't say that if you were to die, I don't want a good life. If you die then dammit, I might as well too! You are the only thing I've ever felt was right in my life! I know I've only known you for a couple days…"

"Length of time doesn't matter. If your life is destined to be intertwined with mine then time will tell, but if you feel that way. I guess you can stick around for a little while." He chuckles but speaks with a sincere tone.

"Honestly, you're an ass." She says smiling and chuckling. "Hey, Levi."

"Something the matter?"

"When you're no longer on the run, can you not wear a helmet anymore?"

"Why? I like my helmet; it protects me from strikes to the head."

"Well… You're."

"What?"

"You're just handsome… that's all. That was the first time I have seen your face and I liked it… I guess."

"Oh, we are doing compliments now?"

"Shut up! I am just saying you look good without the helmet, that is all."

"Then I guess I can say that you are very beautiful, Estelle." Estelle turns her head quickly towards Levi, her face is beat red, and a smile is peeking through. Levi looks back at her as her amethyst eyes twinkle in the moonlight. "Especially your eyes."

"Is that why you looked at me on the mountain?"

"Something like that."

"You are an ass."

"What did I say?"

The two chuckle and laugh as the horse trots steadily down the snow-covered path. Their day has taken a toll on Estelle and Levi both, the rest of their ride is in silence as they ride through the night, bundled together in warmth under the cloak Levi had given to Estelle when they first met.

In the mountains high above Triveria, Njal and Leif build shelter for their people who are nearing the basecamp for their Northman family.

"Leif, you are the smart one here. How long should we camp before we attack that kingdom?"

"Well, I wouldn't say we wait much longer. Perhaps another few days, a week at most. I have taken steady note of their armies' movement and their routines. A little more information would be helpful, but every single one of us might die either way, so who can say."

"Well good, I'm getting restless just waiting here." Njal says placing the final piece of the large log shelter on the rooftop as if it were just a twig.

"The others should be arriving shortly, we'll speak with Sweyn when he arrives, and he can make the final call. Who knows, he might say to return home."

"Ha! Our King would have our heads if we returned. He sent us here with a message to this lofty Kingdom, and I'm excited to deliver it." He says dusting the snow from his gloves.

"You're always bullheaded, but I like the spirit." Leif says with a chuckle.

The two men stand watching over the mountains for their counterparts, in the distance. A large group of men and women are walking steadily through the deep snow, you can see their cheerful laughter and excitement as if it is time for a celebration as they get closer. Their numbers nearing two hundred strong, to the fifty thousand strong of the Triverian army seem almost incomparable. But the burliness and threatening aura that every single one gives off appears to deliver a powerful message. They will not fall.

The room containing the stone legend in the great castle of Triveria flickers with a dim blue light. The stone changes back to its previous shape, the flower crown has reappeared around the wolf's head, yet the Mark of the Boar has begun glowing red as if it were burning within the pits of hell all on its own.

"It seems the time of ruin is upon us." A shadowed figure says from the opening in the door. His old frail voice creeks inside of the empty room along with the sound of the flickering torches. "How odd." He says approaching the stone legend. "The Boar has begun glowing red. I have witnessed a millennium come and pass, though I have never seen this happen before. How odd. Perhaps Ankore is nearing his limit of control, that makes it a little easier than I expected." He says with a devious smile before turning and walking out of the room. As he does, the raven begins to glow dimly with an orange glow as well, as if it were to be the next to turn.

Chapter 6: The Torches of War

As the morning sun rises over the sea to the east of Drixyl, Captain Ankore is the first to wake his platoon in Drixyl. He sits up in his cot and turns to the side setting his feet over the side of his bed. He looks down at his hands for a moment, noticing the mark he bears on his left wrist, the Mark of the Boar is scarred, around the black outline of it. Almost like his skin was burned with a brand through the evening. He stands, ignoring the change to his mark and gathers his clothing and armor placed on a canvas sack containing his gear. Captain Ankore's taken hold in a former store in Drixyl, while his soldiers camp in the cold outskirts of town in thin tents and deep snow.

In the bathroom hangs a mirror just above a metal basin used as a sink, Captain Ankore stands in front of it holding his arms on the metal pot looking into his own eyes in the mirror. Silence rings through his ears and a vicious scowl cements itself on his brow. In a fit of anger, he yells and punches the mirror in front of him, shattering it into a million pieces as it falls to the ground. "Why have you forced me to come this far, brother. Why have you taken me from the Kingdom, why have you forsaken our family, and why have you caused my hands to be stained in blood, over the woman you say you loved. You did this, you made me this way, you made me a murderer, a cold, heartless murderer." Captain Ankore winces in pain. "Fuck!" He yells, holding his bleeding hand and wrapping it in a towel that was hanging on a wall. Captain Ankore turns and sees a woman standing in the doorway watching as he bandages his hand. "Where did you come from!?" He yells.

"I'm sorry, I heard glass break and I came in to see if everything was okay."

"Forgive my tone. I do not mean to lash out at you like that. I must ask you to leave me be. I am perfectly fine."

"You are not fine. Your hand is cut open."

"I said leave me be woman!" Captain Ankore yells in anger.

"Let me see it." She insists, with a quick movement, Captain Ankore strikes the woman across the face and she falls to the ground crying and yelling in pain.

"I told you to leave me be!" He says stepping over her. As he walks through the former store, he knocks over the wooden shelves and stands in the storefront staring out to the streets. A group of townsfolk are watching intently, hearing the commotion from inside the makeshift home. He matches their stare with the same scowl as he gave the mirror.

Captain Ankore walks out of his temporary home into the snow-covered streets of Drixyl. "What are you looking at? Begone peasants!" He yells, striking fear in the group's minds. He slowly looks around him, turning in a full circle. "Levi! Come out here! Face me like a man! Coward! You bastard! AHHH!" He yells, as a green aura of energy appears around him, though it is unstable and fluttering unlike a standard aura of magic that would appear when a user casts a spell. He turns and walks towards the outskirts of Drixyl where the soldiers are, leaving a trail of blood from his now unwrapped wound.

The early morning brings a slow snowfall over the valleys and forests around Vorchid, the ships are steadily being loaded and unloaded at each dock along the river through Vorchid, preparing for their next destination. A few workers are arguing with a man dressed in a long fur coat wearing jewelry made of gold and embedded with precious gems that shimmer from the glow of the flowing water.

"We demand higher pay; we are working day after day for under the average wage of a field worker!" One of the men yells towards the wealthy man in fur.

"I will not pay you a single copper more, you do not deserve even what I am giving you at this moment. If you do not like that then begone, I will find workers that will work for half the cost of you lot."

"This will not be the last you see of us. This is a warning, Mr. Averey…" One man dressed in what appears to be rags and canvas says viciously.

"Begone you peasants. You can forget about your pay for today as well." He says walking onto his large oak ship.

Kristoff is on the street above watching the interaction closely, trying to grasp the reasoning behind the confrontation. Levi and Estelle are just behind him, seemingly arguing playfully over something.

"Would you two be quiet!? I'm busy!" Kristoff turns and yells.

"Is that what you call it?" Levi asks jokingly.

"Oh, shut up. Let us go. We must go see Ms. Ryker this morning. Maria insisted we not be unpunctual with our arrival." He says turning and walking. He has changed from his armor from the Fourth Edict into casual winter clothing. Estelle has changed as well into something similar, but still wearing Levi's cloak. Levi, on the other hand, is still wearing his rotten armor and dirty helmet.

"Levi, you need new armor. We should go find a blacksmith before we see Isabella. It would be rude to meet with her wearing something so… disgusting."

Levi looks down and examines himself. "What's wrong with my armor?"

"Seriously? Half of it is missing, even your sword has gotten in such dreadful condition that you should be embarrassed even wielding it." Kristoff scoffs.

"Fine, I saw one on the way to Isabella's homestead the other day. We can go there first."

"Perfect." Estelle says, taking Levi's arm and pulling him quickly to catch up to Kristoff.

The trio traverse the busy morning streets of the merchant town of Vorchid, Levi and Kristoff are paying close attention as they walk past each merchant. Examining their prices as well as the amount of poverty that is riddling the streets.

Kristoff shakes his head in disbelief as he walks past. "I'm surprised these people can even afford food; do you see some of these prices?"

"Maria mentioned that everyone here is becoming more and more greedy with each day that passes. I wonder what that's all about."

"Levi, do you think it has something to do with the structure in Kreitor? My book said that the Ox symbol bears the weight of the world's avarice. That means greed, right?"

"Yes. In fact, it is greed to the utmost highest degree. Wait a second, the Prince was born with the Mark of the Ox was he not?"

"Yes, he was. Maybe Maria will have more insight."

"Did you two know the Prince?"

"Yes, we both did. He was just a little older than us, a bit insufferable though." Kristoff says.

"A bit? I could not stand the guy. He was the most annoying person I've ever met, always flashing his jewelry like he earned it himself."

"You always did hold a bit of resentment towards him."

"Do you two know any more of the Sacred Six?" Estelle asks curiously.

"Yes, we knew all of them." Kristoff answers happily.

"That is amazing, what are they like?"

"Hit or miss. They're just normal people for the most part." Levi says.

"Oh, I would expect them to be distinguished."

"Does she not know that Levi is one of the six?" Kristoff thinks to himself.

"We are here. Do you two need anything?" Levi asks.

"No, my armor and weaponry are fine."

Estelle thinks to herself for a moment before answering. "I could use some armor."

"Oh, Estelle. Did Johnathan give you the gold and deliver the message I asked him to?"

"Yes, I almost forgot. Here is your gold back." She says pulling a small bag of gold from her satchel.

"No, it is yours. Buy new armor. I do not need it."

"Look at Mr. Moneybags over here, where did you get all of your money?" Kristoff chuckles.

"I have been busy since I left the Kingdom."

"Busy, huh? Working the street corners?"

"Very funny." Levi says opening the door to the blacksmith's shop.

Inside of the shop is just like you would expect from a blacksmith, except the prices are outrageous compared to a normal blacksmith in any other town. The quality of the work is on par with an experienced craftsman's and the forge radiating a comforting heat that feels as if it is warming the soul of the trio.

"What can I do for you, young man!?" A stocky dwarven man asks Levi enthusiastically as he comes around from the corner of the desk.

"I'd like new armor, and a new sword."

"Alright, strip down come with me. I'll take some measurements." He says returning behind the desk. "I'll be with you two in a few minutes. Just hold your horses." He says to Estelle and Kristoff who look at each other in confusion because of the Dwarves' odd manners. Levi takes his armor off and places it on the desk before following the dwarven man.

Estelle and Kristoff take their time walking around the shop, examining the crafted pieces of equipment. Kristoff draws a finely crafted sword made from a sheath sitting on a stand, admiring the craftsmanship for a moment before looking at the price tag and promptly placing it back on the shelf carefully, and backing away slowly. Estelle on the other hand, is picking up an armful of items such as new blades, a new bow, a new quiver full of arrows, and a few pieces of armor.

"Estelle, can you afford all that? This place is rather pricey."

"Yes, Levi gave me one hundred gold pieces for the basilisk contract and instructed me to get new armor and equipment."

"One hundred gold!?"

"Yes, crazy isn't it? I do not know where he managed to get all of this money just to give away."

"Levi has always been frugal about most things unless impulse takes control. I can imagine being on the run he tried to not make a paper trail for the Knights to follow."

"He did say he lives from the land and barely goes into stores."

"That sounds like what he would do. I would do the same thing."

"How long have you known Levi?" Estelle asks curiously.

"Oh, I believe we met... perhaps fifteen years ago. My, I did not realize it has been that long."

"Wow, so you two are close, I am taking it?"

"Of course, we are like brothers. We did everything together most of the time."

"Can you tell me about him? Figuring him out is like trying to decipher an ancient rune."

"Sure, what do you want to know?"

"What is his deal? Why's he so quiet and serious all the time?"

"He hasn't had a very easy life, even being a member of the Six. His father passed away when he was in his teenage years, and his mother died at birth. After he was adopted by order of the Queen to another member of the Six's family. The Captain of the platoon's family in fact. They are adoptive brothers. The tragedy and loss he has felt in life made him distant and cold to everyone, I am rather shocked he is even willing to joke with you about anything. It took me a while to open him up."

"Wait a second. Levi's a member of the Sacred Six?"

"Oh, he hasn't told you. Yes. He bears the Mark of the Wolf."

"The Wolf…" Estelle says, looking over top of the desk towards the forge where Levi is standing towards the back of the wall while the dwarf takes measurements.

"He has always been quiet about it, he is not one to boast, nor brag about anything. He just lives and let's live. I believe that is why we get along so well."

"You said Captain Ankore… was it? Is Levi's adoptive brother?"

"Yes, they've never got along well. Levi's always been better at basically everything, school, swordsmanship, intelligence, and handling life in general. It has given Theo an inferiority complex that spawned from the jealousy welling deep inside of him."

"Is that why he executed Johnathan?"

Kristoff turns his head towards Estelle, placing his hand on his soft fur covered chin. "Most likely, he has been on a warpath and needs to be stopped sooner rather than later. I fear a climax is coming from the pent-up anger Levi has withheld and the unruly jealousy that Theo has had his entire life. He has torn through town after town like a wild beast pillaging everything in its wake. I assumed you knew where Levi was, that is why I decided it best to leave the platoon now."

"Alright, look in the mirror out there. See if you like it." The Dwarven man says to Levi happily, proud of his craftsmanship.

Levi walks out of the back wearing newly forged plate armor, all new moleskin boots and gauntlets, as well as a new helmet nearly identical to his first but this one's horns are sharper, and made of a black metal alloy with blue rings from the scorching hot forge instead of the previous silver. His helmet no longer covers his entire face, perhaps to appease Estelle's request. Instead it is more open, though much more menacing. The spalder on his right shoulder has two similar horns curving up towards the sky as well. Along with the exquisite detail of the plate armor, there are also several runes engraved into the metal. Though, they seem to be in an ancient language.

Levi examines his armor and moves his arms and legs to test his ability to move. "This will work, I will take it. I need a sword too."

"What size would you like? You're a decent size guy, two handed or one handed?"

"One handed, thirty-seven or thirty-nine inches."

"A little longer than most, hold on. I have just the thing for you." He says returning to his forge and reaching into an oak and steel chest on the floor. He pulls a finely wrapped sword from the bottom of the chest and blows the dust from the cover. "How is something like this?" He says handing the sword to Levi. He unwraps it and draws it from its sheath. The blade is a finely crafted steel, with a black inlay directly forged into the center of the blade. "It is my masterpiece of craftsmanship. I made oh, thirty years ago and no one desired the size. But it is exactly thirty-eight-inch blade with a hilt precisely forged for single handed use. The black wrap around the hilt is a special material I came across, crafted from griffin skin and yetari fur and infused with a bonding magic. It is the most durable and tactile sword you will ever use." Levi takes a few quick swings, getting a feel for the weight and length.

"Perfect. I will take it."

"Wonderful. I am glad someone is going to enjoy my finest craftsmanship after all these years. Oh, and the runes on the blade, they will glow with whatever distribution of magic you concentrate into them. Offensive will glow red, nature will glow green, et cetera et cetera. The runes translate to A King is nothing more than the warrior under his rule. I engraved that back in the day too, when I was all feisty with the elven kingdom, but that is all in the past."

"How much for everything, and her stuff too?"

"Oh, my. We have got a wealthy one in here, come here young lady... wait a damn minute." He says walking from around the desk and out onto the floor of his shop. He stops in front of Estelle and adjusts his glasses and rubs his beard, eyeing her up momentarily. "Estelle? Is that you? My you look so grown up! I did not even recognize you!"

"Lok! I thought it was you, but I was not sure! Oh, how have you been!" Estelle cheerfully answers, giving him a hug.

"Oh, you know, I've been busy. How about you? What are you doing all the way up here?"

"Nothing too special, I just decided to travel and learn more about the world."

"That is wonderful my dear, just absolutely wonderful. A future Queen with culture under her belt is what the Kingdom of Fellistar needs. Let me take that stuff for you, is there anything else you would like? On the house! Anything for the princess!"

"Lok, I insist. Let me pay."

"Not a chance young lady, this old man still pays respect to royalty no matter how rotten my mind has become."

"Well, thank you, Lok. That'll be it." Lok wraps the armor into a carrying bag along with a sheath for the sword for Estelle.

"Estelle, do you know this young man?"

"Yes, care to give him a discount?"

"Of course! He can get the same discount as I am giving you. Free of charge young man, come back and see me sometime. I will brew some tea."

"Sir, might I ask you something." Kristoff says with an inquisitive tone.

"Certainly."

"Don't take offense, but why are the prices in the shop…well outrageous?" The old dwarf grumbles under his breath for a moment before answering.

"Back in the day, I had the best prices in town. But the price of material went through the roof recently. I understand supply and demand, but ten gold pieces for an ingot of steel? Ridiculous. These merchants are becoming more and more greedy, I do not quite understand it. They have a steady supply of material yet wish to charge an arm and a leg for something as miniscule as a single ingot."

"Interesting." Kristoff says, rubbing the fur on his chin.

"It is like they've all caught a bug of some sort, a money grub." He laughs at his own trite joke hysterically.

"Alright, we're off." Levi says as he walks towards the door.

"Goodbye, Lok! I will stop back in and chat when I have some free time!" Estelle says with a smile and wave as the trio exits the shop.

"Levi, I have a feeling the excessive greed within this town has something to do with the death of the prince, at first it was a hunch, but I do not know anymore. I do not tend to believe in legends, but this does not make sense."

"That is what I was thinking." Levi says. "We should hurry and inform Maria of our experience in the town."

"Right."

"Hey, Levi."

"Something wrong Estelle?"

"How come you did not tell me you were one of the Sacred Six?" Levi stops suddenly and turns his head towards Kristoff, who continues to walk but starts to whistle as if he has no role in the conversation.

"It's not very important, it is nothing more than a fancy birthmark."

"Mmm, sure." Estelle says, walking past Levi with a hint of annoyance in her voice. "Got any more secrets you want to tell?" Levi remains silent and shakes his head as he continues walking after Estelle and Kristoff.

Kristoff is the first to enter the immaculate estate that Isabella Ryker calls her home, she and Maria are sitting beside one another discussing the events that took place within Kreitor over a glass of wine. As Kristoff walks in he feels his gut drop, as if something is telling him to turn around and walk out at that very instant. He disregards his feelings, shaking his head and clearing his throat. Levi and Estelle are the next to enter, bickering playfully because Levi is refusing to remove his helmet purposely, just to annoy Estelle.

"They are here, great. I need to speak with Levi immediately." Isabella says, standing and walking into the hallway to greet everyone. "Come this way everyone, we have much to discuss." She says hastily bringing the trio into the office.

Njal is perched atop a mountain looking outward towards the ocean past Triveria, watching as a white wall of snow overtakes the scenic ocean view a little ways out in the water. He looks to the sky and takes note of the wind and clouds steadily moving their way, he nods and stands from his perch.

In the camp of Northmen that Njal and Leif built high in the mountains, men and women join in a feast. Drinking barrels of wine and devouring a multitude of different animals they harvested from the mountain region. Through the laughter and chatter of the packed long hut, a feeling of excitement continues to grow within the mind of each person's mind.

Njal soon joins the crowded hut with a smile on his face, a group of men and women call out to him to join their festivities. Before he can take a seat, he is stopped by a large burly man and pulled towards the side of the hut.

"Njal, what did the ocean foretell?"

"A large snowstorm will be hitting the shore in the night. It will be a blizzard, perhaps it will be best to make our move before the sun rises. The soldiers will not have time to prepare for the weather, but we will be ready. Have you created a plan with the information I've collected, Sweyn?"

"Yes, I have. Thankfully, the chieftain sent more of our people, the size of that fortress would be far more troublesome with the original plan of one hundred. We will advance in the early morning just before sunrise, we will spread ourselves into groups of five and pillage the Kingdom. The five of us should be worth one hundred of them. But that will be discussed later, go eat your fill, this may very well be one of our last meals."

"Aye, we will march into the gates with the blood of a thousand men soaked into our boots."

The morning in Triveria is an especially cold one because of the icy air blowing in from the roaring, icy ocean to the east. The King stands atop the balcony outside of his throne room overlooking his bustling Kingdom, the Knights are making their morning rounds, the townsfolk are shopping, and the children are playing in the snow. A tear falls down his face as he watches closely. The Queen steps out from the open glass door and wraps a thick cloak around herself. The cold wind blows her pearly white hair towards the side, though her hair signifies age, one would not say she looked a day over thirty. Her skin is smooth, and free of wrinkles entirely, though she is nearing her late fifties. She steps next to her King, wrapping the cloak around him as well and resting her head on his shoulder. Noticing the tears slowly falling down his face.

"Markor, what's wrong?"

"I am just worried, my dear."

"Of what, what could be wrong?"

"I am worried the demon will bring ruin to this Kingdom, and there is nothing I can do to stop his impending destruction."

"Markor, I do not believe that Levi would do something like that. He was always a sweet boy."

"He murdered our son! And you have the audacity to refer to him so... endearingly?!"

"I do not believe our son was murdered by Levi, the report from that day makes no sense."

"Makes no sense!? He was standing over our sons' body! His hands and body covered in the blood of my dear boy. And when he was accused, he could not even speak to defend himself!"

"Does that not cause concern?"

"What!?"

"That he could not speak. Does something not seem amiss here?"

"I do not know, my dear. I am sorry for raising my voice, I just..."

"It is fine, the loss of our first born was hard on us both. It is alright to let your emotions sometimes." She says hugging him tightly.

"I must do something; I cannot just sit back and watch as my Kingdom falls to ruin. I pray to the Lord that Ankore can follow through with the orders and bring the demon to me. The council guaranteed me that my Kingdom will be safe if he is brought to them alive, along with some woman they called the Amaranthine."

"The Amaranthine?"

"Yes, the legend says the Wolf is drawn to the Amaranthine. Wherever she goes he will follow once he first catches her scent."

"That word... it means the undying flower. Why is she called that?"

"I do not know. I regret not following through with my plan nine years ago. I should have

executed that demon the moment I was warned."
The Queen stands in silence, remembering the day
as if it were happening just before her eyes once
again. She is caught in a daze as the images of the
King killing Levi's father flash before her eyes.
"Come inside, there is a storm approaching from
the east. It is going to freeze the air soon." The King
says, walking with his Queen back in from the
balcony and locking the large glass doors behind
them.

Yelling and cries of sorrow disturb the
homestead of Isabella's, the men at work on the
rooftop stop and listen closely. The sound of glass
breaking and a woman yelling murder shocks them
for a moment, they all shake their heads and
continue their work steadily as the commotion
ensues.

"Murderers! All of you! I will have your
heads! You are filthy, worthless vermin!"

"Bella! Please calm down, it is not Kristoff's doing. He abandoned the Triverian army and is with us now!"

Maria holds Isabella back from gouging Kristoff's eyes out. "I do not care! I will have his head!"

Kristoff is crouching behind a wooden table that he has flipped on its side, covering his head as expensive vases and glassware fly over him. "Miss, please, I beg of you. I tried to defend your brother, I tried to stop the cruelty. I swear on my life! But I could not do it alone!"

"Isabella, if you wish to blame someone for Johnathan's death. Please, blame me. He helped me escape from Drixyl, telling me to find you. I am at fault, if I would have stood up to the knights, he would still be here." Levi says, a tone of sorrow overcomes his normally stern voice.

Bella's anger fades from a vicious ferocity to an ocean of anger as tears fall down her face, streaming her black eyeliner down along with each tear. "I want your leader's head brought to me!"

"Isabella, that is a death sentence. The soldiers in the platoon are all held at the highest skill and ranking within the Triverian army. Each one as ruthless as the next." Kristoff pleas.

Isabella calms down a little more, regaining her composure and sitting down and laying her head back on the luxurious leather soft. "Then we will bring them here, my guards far outnumber them. We will slaughter them all like the pigs they are."

"Bella, we cannot do that. I have known Captain Ankore most of my life, he is a ruthless savage in battle. He will kill any person in town that stands in his way of finding Levi." Maria says, sitting down next to Bella. Estelle is sitting next to Levi, and Yovanna is sitting quietly as the conversation continues.

"I have an idea; I am due to return from tailing Estelle and Yovanna with a member of my squad. He is nearly the same build as Levi, we can disguise ourselves and infiltrate Drixyl. Perhaps Levi and I can strike while we are in disguise."

"Can you get close to him?"

"The Captain? Yes. He has taken hold in an abandoned store in Drixyl. The rest of the platoon camps outside of the town. Perhaps we can return with Estelle and Yovanna as hostages to better suit our disguises. It's better than returning empty handed."

"Are you two alright with that?" Bella asks Estelle and Yovanna.

"I am ready!" Estelle says with excitement in her voice.

"No. It will be too dangerous if a fight breaks out." Levi says, interrupting the conversation.

"Levi's right. If Ankore realizes what is going on. It could turn bad in an instant. They would be surrounded by every knight in Drixyl.

"I'm willing to take the risk. Johnathan did not need to be treated like that; he did not deserve it. He always treated me so courteously." Estelle's face is overcome with a look of sorry as her tone drops.

"I am okay with it too. I'm sure Levi and Kristoff will be able to protect us, even if things go bad." Yovanna says, smiling kindly at Kristoff, causing him to choke up a little bit.

"Levi, I am sorry, but we are going through with this. I am sorry to ask you to go into the den of the dragon, but I demand vengeance for my brother." Levi is silent for a moment, looking around at the group and stopping at Estelle for a moment.

"Alright, we will leave at once. If we leave now, we can be there just before sundown, we will be able to escape in the night easier."

"Then it is settled. We are off to hunt a monster." Kristoff says, looking at Levi with a generous smile as a reminiscent feeling of past adventures overcomes their minds.

"Let us hope we come back alive; I am sure my brother's been holding back a lot of anger towards me since I ran from the Kingdom."

"I am sure it will be fine, no reason to tarry, let us get at it." The group stands from their seats and proceeds towards the door out of Isabella's homestead.

"Maria, would you mind staying here for a moment. I have some other business that requires attention."

"Oh, certainly. Come back safe everyone, I will see you soon." Maria says with a smile, closing the door behind Yovanna, who is the last to exit.

"Alright everyone, Kristoff and I will ready the horses and change into the scout's armor. We will meet at the front gate near Maria's home shortly. Be sure to wear the same things you did when you left Drixyl, it's a must that we all appear to be the same as we did once we left."

"Okay, no problem." Estelle says confidently. "Oh crap, what was I wearing..." She says under her breath.

"You were wearing a green and brown tunic with knee high boots over your black leather pants. You also had my cloak, and your hair was tied into a braid on the right side." Levi says without skipping a beat.

"Seems you have paid close attention to her, Levi." Kristoff chuckles.

"That was pretty good! What was I wearing, Levi?" Yovanna asks.

"Oh, um." Levi hesitates shortly. "Oh, look at the time. We must hurry now. Meet us at the gate soon." Levi says, pulling Kristoff along down the street towards the gate.

"Seems like he is a little interested in you." Yovanna chuckles with a cheeky smile. Estelle's face turns red with a heavy blush.

"He is just considerate, that is all."

"Uh, huh. Come on, let us go get ready."

Maria and Bella are sitting in a study, wall to wall with books and stacks of papers all over the numerous tables in the room. Calling the room unorganized cannot begin to describe the state of the room. Though it radiates a calming scent of old written work and spilled ink, relaxing to all, despite the sight.

"Maria, are you aware of the current situation to the fullest extent?"

"What do you mean?"

"It seems as though; Estelle is a little more than infatuated with Levi from what you've told me. But her friend, Yovanna, is a little conspicuous."

"I've noticed that. I am not sure about Estelle; she is awfully friendly with Levi. Though I do not care for it, I do not believe she is a reason for concern towards Levi's safety."

"We will see about that. Yovanna on the other hand, she had a Triverian opal around her neck."

"What? I had not noticed. That is primarily used by the Triverian Army as a communication stone."

"If you remember correctly, Kristoff has five gems lined into his left gauntlet. A topaz, sapphire, amethyst, emerald, and ruby. All bearing the Triverian star in the center. I am rather worried this could lead to something a bit more troublesome. I need you to find Levi and Kristoff, speak to them privately and warn them that either of those girls may be in cohorts with the Triverian knights. I did

not notice anything on Estelle but still be cautious.

The only way for them to discover the truth is if

Ankore has the partner stone."

"Perhaps Estelle may have some connection

as well. When she first found Levi and I, she was

with Yovanna. Perhaps it would be best to avoid

any chances at a time like this. I will hurry now and

speak with them."

"Be careful, Maria." Bella says, taking a worn

book from the shelf and flipping through it quickly.

Maria hurries through the busy streets of

Drixyl, the skies are clear, and the sun is shining

brightly through the streets but the cold wind from

the flowing river nearby counters the warming

light. The streets are deteriorating, instead of

cheerful bartering and people laughing like normal.

The patrons are arguing with the merchants over

their prices, refusing to pay, and some even swiping

goods and running away through the fast-moving

crowds. Guards are watching closely, but not

bothering with the thefts as they themselves seem to disagree with the merchant's exorbitant prices.

"Kristoff!" Maria yells out to the two men in black Triverian armor. They turn and Kristoff happily waves. "Kristoff, where are the girls?"

"Oh, they are getting ready. They should be here soon."

"Oh, thank goodness. Kristoff let me see your gauntlet, you too Levi."

"Okay, what is this about?" Kristoff asks curiously, Maria pulls his arm and quickly examines the stone fragments embedded into his gauntlet. "No, opal."

"No opal? Of course not, we only use five."

"Kristoff, did you see another stone on Theodore's gauntlet?"

"Yes, he wears seven. These five in addition to a Triverian opal and a black Triverian diamond."

Maria shoves a golden cylinder in Kristoff's face and hands two to Levi. "Here, take these, give this one to Estelle. Do not give one to Yovanna! Do you understand Kristoff, I saw you making lovey-eyes at her earlier?"

Kristoff shakes his head and looks away in embarrassment for a moment before looking back to Maria. "Yes, yes fine. What are these?"

"Do not worry about it, just press the silver button on this if any trouble arises. Do you understand, the silver button!" Maria says, running off back into the busy crowds, gone as quickly as she appeared.

"Are you boys ready?" Estelle says running with Yovanna towards the two men dressed in the armor of the Fourth Edict with excitement in her voice.

"Yes. Hurry now." Kristoff says. "Sorry about this, but we are going to have to tie your hands together. We must make the ruse seem believable." Levi takes a small length of rope from Kristoff and nods towards Estelle to come closer. The men tie Estelle and Yovanna hands together loosely.

"Is that alright, Estelle? I am not hurting you, am I?"

"No, that is fine. But, how are we going to get onto the horses?" She asks, looking at the horse's back towering above her. Levi looks at the horse, then back at Estelle.

"Oh damn, should have thought ahead a little bit." Kristoff says.

"It's no trouble." Levi says, he grabs Estelle around the waist, turning her face red instantly as she has never experienced the firm touch of a man prior to this moment. Levi lifts her onto the horse with ease, as if she is as light as a feather.

"Well, that is one way of doing it." Kristoff chuckles and looks at Estelle. "Look what you've done, Levi. You have made her blush. Her face is red enough to light the way." He laughs and looks at Yovanna. "Alright, your turn."

"Okay." She says, lifting her hands above her head and laughing. Kristoff hoists her high into the air and onto the horse with equal ease, though Yovanna is shorter and smaller than Estelle in stature.

"Alright, we're off." Levi and Kristoff pat their horses on the shoulder and begin their day's journey towards Drixyl with their ruse unfolding quickly.

"Levi, what did Maria give you?" Estelle peeks over his shoulder and asks curiously.

"Oh, right. Here keep this on you if things go south press the silver button. I do not know what it is, or what they do, so do not ask me."

"Okay, got it. If things turn sour press your buttons." She retorts with a chuckle.

"You are a pain." Levi chuckles as a soft wind blows the powdery snow across the field covering the compacted brown snow upon the path.

"Levi, it is best I do the talking, your voice will surely throw Theodore into a fit. Just keep quiet and keep your helmet on."

"Do not worry Kristoff, he's good at that." Estelle half snorts, half giggles.

"Estelle, it will be best if you stop flirting with him and get serious. Ankore is not an idiot, I have been gone for nearly three days as well. This has to go smoothly or else he will have the entire platoon's blades drawn at each of our throats in a moment's notice."

Estelle's face turns red once again, she looks forward with a grin of embarrassment and remains quiet.

"Kristoff, is this Captain guy dangerous?" Yovanna says peeking under Kristoff's arm.

"Dangerous is a peculiar understatement. I have seen him slaughter an entire gaggle of riff raff in a tavern on our journey from the kingdom."

"Oh dear."

"Do not worry, my dear. I will be sure to keep you safe."

"You are sweet, perhaps we can grab a drink after this is over?" Yovanna asks confidently, looking upwards towards Kristoff. Her pearly blue eyes twinkle in the sunlight and the soft wind blowing through the valley careens her hair with a charming flow.

"Did she just ask ME on a date? How odd." Kristoff thinks to himself. "Perhaps, as long as we make it out of Drixyl alive."

"Do not worry. I'm sure we will all be safe." She says confidently.

The sun skims the skyline as the day passes on their journey. Just before it kisses the mountain tops their horses trot through the northern gate of

Drixyl. The townsfolk quickly scurry into their home. The presence of the platoon has made them step with caution after the public execution of their beloved guild master. As the horses' trot into the center of town, Levi's eyes are scarred with the sight of Johnathan's frozen corpse. Still hanging from the gallows, the very same as when his life was cut short. Levi draws his horse to a stop abruptly, staring at the corpse swaying in the wind as it blows through town.

"Levi, are you okay?" Estelle asks, peeking around Levi and seeing Johnathan hanging as well. "Dear Lord..." She says covering her mouth with her tied hands. Levi is silent. Staring at the corpse while sitting motionless on his horse. Estelle feels his breathing become sporadic, as if he were stricken by a chaotic notion.

"Levi..." Estelle nudges Levi on the shoulder. Snapping him out of daze. He shakes his head and continues through town, catching up with Kristoff and Yovanna. "Are you alright?" She asks, though Levi does not answer. "It is not your fault, don't blame yourself." She whispers.

More civilians run into their homes and stores as they pass.

"We are here." Kristoff says, dismounting his horse and lifting Yovanna from it. Levi follows suit and lifts Estelle off, holding her behind him rather than in front as a normal captor would.

Kristoff knocks on the door where Ankore has taken hold. The heavy metal gauntlet knocks loudly against the hardwood door. He steps back and waits. Kristoff feels his heart sink into his stomach. His nerves take over, though he tries to remain calm. Levi and Estelle are standing next to him, waiting as metal boot's stomp against a hardwood floor. In an instant, the door swings open. Captain Ankore stands silently for a moment, staring viciously at the four standing at his door. He nods his head to the rear and holds the door for them as they all enter.

"Sit." Ankore points to wooden chairs around a long table. The floor is covered in broken glass and wood chips from his previous outburst of anger. The four-follow suit and take their seats. Levi and Kristoff move the chairs out in the center for the two women, and then take their seats next to them on each side. "Untie their hands." Ankore paces back and forth in front of the table for a moment then steps into the next room for a moment. He returns with four glasses and a large bottle of wine, filling the glasses nearly halfway. He stares at each of them silently as he pours.

"We had no luck finding..." Kristoff looks towards his Captain.

"Quiet. I do not wish to hear you speak." The Captain stands at the front of the table, watching them closely.

Levi is sitting patiently, not looking towards his brother, nor giving him attention when he peers through his soul. From the streets, Levi hears a flurry of metal and stomping approach from the south.

"Good, they are here." Ankore draws his sword and places the tip on Levi's throat, causing him to look up instantly.

"Sir! Why are you doing..."

"Silence!" Ankore yells viciously.

"Levi. Do you believe me to be a fool!? Do you believe you can simply walk into this town and I would not notice you! I know my own brother the moment I see him! Helmet or no! Give me a reason! One reason! I should not end your miserable life at this instant!"

"Stop!" Estelle yells, standing from her chair, knocking it over completely.

"Silence!" Captain Ankore yells, turning his attention to Estelle. He draws his fist towards her. Before he can move a muscle, Levi strikes the sword away from his throat and lunges towards Captain Ankore.

"I will not let you harm them!" Levi punches Ankore in the jaw causing him to fall along with Levi on top of him. Their armor clangs repeatedly as they roll on the floor, striking each other, with each blow having the intent to kill. Kristoff jumps from his seat and draws his blade, with the intent to end the scuffle quickly. Before he can take a step, the door slams open. The knights begin pouring into the small store, each with their weapon drawn and ready to defend their Captain. Levi is thrown backwards from the ground towards the door.

"Kill him! Kill him now!" Ankore yells, trying to stand.

"Levi!" Estelle rushes towards Levi. Kristoff presses a button on the device Maria has given him repeatedly. "What the hell does this thing do!"

"Estelle!" Levi says lunging towards Estelle in an attempt to dodge a piercing strike from Arthur, the largest member of the Fourth Edict. Before Levi can escape, Arthur's blade slices through the opening in the rear of his armor.

Piercing completely through his calf and sticking into the ground. Levi winces in pain, letting out an ear-piercing scream of pain. Levi locks his fingers around Estelle's ankle and in an instant a blue glow flashes in the room. Levi and Estelle vanish as if they were never there.

Arthur pulls his blade that is driven deep into the wood floor and turns his glare directly towards Kristoff. Kristoff begins to panic, ferociously tapping the button on the device. He looks down. Arthur raises his blade readying a fatal blow to Kristoff.

"Damnit! Wrong button!"

As Arthur's sword comes striking down like a bolt of lightning, just before slicing Kristoff's head into two he vanishes within a flash of white light. The thunderous crack of Arthur's sword striking deep into the wooden table clears the commotion in the room. Captain Ankore stands and wipes the blood from his face.

"Where did they go!?" He yells looking towards Yovanna angrily.

"They must have returned to Vorchid." She says calmly, sipping her wine as if nothing happened.

"How!?" Ankore wipes off more of the blood streaming down his face.

"It seems that Maria was plotting behind my back. I am not sure how she found out I was spying though. I was discreet about it the entire time."

"That's how! You worthless imbecile! That opal you parade around your throat has the Triverian star directly on it! Damnit!" Captain Ankore yells and slaps Yovanna from her chair, shattering the wine glass she was holding in her hand. She begins to cry, holding her face in pain.

"I am sorry! I did not realize anyone would notice!" She pleas with a muffled voice through her cry.

"Give me that!" Ankore rips the chained opal from her neck, pulling her upward causing her head to slam from the ground. "You are as worthless as a spy as you are as a mate! Give me my sword!" He extends his hand, looking at Yovanna with rage in his eyes with blood streaming down his face from Levi's blows still. Arthur hands him his sword willfully and watches silently. He raises his arm to strike Yovanna, but Kristoff appears the same as he left the first time with a flash of white light, disorienting the soldiers in the room causing Captain Ankore to release Yovanna.

"Sorry to intrude, I forgot something." He says chuckling nonchalantly as if he did not walk into the gates of hell. Kristoff takes Yovanna's hand and presses the silver button on his device once again. The entire room is in shock over the events that just took place.

Captain Ankore lets out a blood curdling yell, both of pain and anger. He strikes the wooden wall, driving his fist through it completely.

"Captain, should we advance on Vorchid?" Arthur asks in his deep monotone voice.

"No, not yet. We need reinforcements." Captain Ankore takes a white towel and holds it over his face walking past the soldiers. "Return to your camp. I will contact the Kingdom and give you all updates the moment I have a plan together."

Maria is tapping her foot on the ground nervously and pacing back and forth across the hardwood floor. The click of her heels echo through the spacious hallways. Suddenly the room is filled with a bright white light, almost as bright as the sun it seems. Kristoff appears as the light fades, along with Yovanna, who is lying on the ground holding her face.

"Honestly, what a handy trick that is. Poof, gone in an instant. That would have been nice a time or two before."

"Shut up, Kristoff! Where is Levi!?"

"Oh, right. I do not know. He was not there, so I just grabbed her and came back. Almost lost my life trying to save this woman."

"You! You bitch! Where is Levi!?"

"I do not know! He disappeared with Estelle using magic!"

"Dammit! Why did he not use the device I gave him?"

"Well, he was in a bit of a pinch. Likely did not have time to get it ready. When he was rolling around on the floor with his brother, he might have broken it too. But not to worry, Estelle had one as well did she not?" Kristoff crosses his arms and asks Maria, his tone seemingly calming down now. Maria begins pacing back and forth again. "Maria?"

"What!?" She exclaims in frustration.

"Calm yourself, Estelle had one of these fancy things as well."

"Yes, but hers was not real! It was purely a means to keep Levi's mouth shut about them."

"What do you mean hers wasn't real?"

"I do not know if we can trust her, so I gave her a fake hoping to leave her in Drixyl for the time being."

"You were going to leave that girl in the middle of that hornet's nest? For what? Because she was getting along with Levi! Let go of your infatuation with him, years have passed, it is time to move on!" Kristoff yells now flush with anger. Maria extends her arm and slaps him across the face. She storms into the next room with her face turning red from anger and embarrassment alike. "That woman is the worst sometimes. You on the other hand, you are the worst all the time it seems. What in the world were you thinking courting with Ankore?" Kristoff lifts Yovanna from the ground onto her feet.

"I thought I could trust him... he saved me from a village outside of the Kingdom two years ago when Bandits set fire to the fields and homes."

"Set fire to the fields? What was the name of this village?"

"The village of Pirah just outside of the great forest."

"Dear lord..." Kristoff says under his breath, rubbing his brow ridge.

"He has struck me before, but only a few times... He always apologizes dearly and tends to my wounds afterward. But this time, it was much harder. He looked as if he wanted to kill me."

"He probably would have, you daft woman! Could you not feel the aura emanating from around him!? He was overflowing with emotions, who knows what he would have done."

"I am sorry..." Kristoff shakes his head and walks into the next room with Maria, leaving

Yovanna to cry on her own, reflecting on the trouble she has caused.

"Maria, I apologize. I let my temper control my tongue. That is very unlike me and I should not have said anything."

"No, no. It is fine, Kristoff. You are right, I need to get over my failures in the past. Do you have any idea where Levi would have taken them to?"

"I do not quite know. He has only ever used that teleportation magic once before with me, we ended up twenty miles past our destination. I doubt he's taken the time to perfect the skill, either."

"Twenty miles? My word, how much energy did Levi put into the spell?"

"Likely every ounce he had within his body. We were caught in an avalanche on Mount Triveria and we nearly died. If he had not used that skill in a moment's notice, we would not be having this conversation today."

"Why was I never told of this?"

"Levi made me promise to keep it between us, he was quite embarrassed by it and likely knew how you would react."

"It is no matter. If Levi put all his energy into the spell, then it's likely that he's gone the same distance if not further."

"Do you have a topographical map of the surrounding area?"

"Yes." Maria pulls a drawer out from her desk and flips through a stack of papers. She pulls out a large canvas sheet and lays it across the mahogany desk. "Okay, teleportation magic only moves matter in a single direction, destination is controlled by energy the user channels into it. He knew the direction of Vorchid, and he was in a pinch you say, so likely he used all of the energy available to him."

"Well, pinch may be an understatement. He had a sword driven through his leg, pinning him to the floor."

"He what!?" Maria exclaims.

"Oh, terribly sorry. Arthur, you remember Arthur, right? Big man, a part of the Fourth Edict. Yes, he stabbed Levi while he was on the ground. Levi tried to move, but he did not dodge it quite well enough."

"Shut up! How is he supposed to survive! You need to find him immediately!" She screams directly in Kristoff's face. "Try to contact him with your gauntlets gemstones!"

"I cannot do that, if I use these the entire platoon in Drixyl will be able to hear every word and they'll be on us quicker than a hungry animal!" He retorts arrogantly. Maria lets out a sigh of anger as she returns to her seat and digs through her drawer to find a ruler. She places it on the map and draws a guiding line along the potential path of Levi's direction.

"They could be anywhere! Ugh!"

"Just give me a direction damnit! Draw a line northwest of Drixyl and give me the damn map!" Kristoff flails his arms in the air.

"Fine! Now go! Hurry!" Maria draws a line directly northwest of the center of Drixyl and hands Kristoff the canvas map.

"You are awfully bossy for someone that caused this entire mess."

"Go!" Maria stands and shoves Kristoff through the doorway. She looks at Yovanna who is sitting in a wooden chair, sobbing in her hands. "For whatever reason Kristoff demanded I send him back to retrieve you is beyond me. But right now, give me the Triverian Opal." She holds her hand out.

"I do not have it. Theodore took it from me when Levi disappeared with Estelle." She sobs, looking up at Maria with her face puffy and eyes bloodshot from crying.

"Dear Lord, look at you. Feeling sorry for yourself, it was your choice getting involved with that incorrigible asshole."

"He saved me! What could I do to repay him!?"

"He did not save you! He was the one who lit the fires and burnt your village to the ground!"

"No! It was the bandits!"

"The bandits have not been near Triveria in over fifty years! Ankore sought to conquer the village of Pirah for the king to try and raise his rank!"

"That is impossible! My family! My mother and father died in the fires!"

"Then blame that man for their deaths!" Maria exclaims in anger, running her fingers through her long curly brunette hair. Yovanna's cries become louder as her mental state begins to deteriorate. Her cries echo through the halls as Maria returns to the desk, deliberating her decisions of the day.

Kristoff hurries through the crowded streets, pushing and shoving his way through. He knocks over a few people along the way but keeps pushing on regardless. He quickly reaches the front gates and mounts a horse hitched just outside. He leaps on the horse and slices the reins tied to the fencepost with his sword before riding off through the snowy fields. A man hurries down the stone road yelling for his horse as Kristoff rides off with the setting sun in his peripheral vision.

Chapter 7: Bury Thy Blade

In a flash of blue light, Levi and Estelle drop from the sky in a deep snowdrift on top of a forested plateau. Levi is groveling on the ground as he loses a copious amount of blood from his leg. Estelle takes a moment to gather herself.

Estelle sits up in the snow and looks around. "Where are we?" She asks Levi, before looking over and panicking. "Levi! Levi! Please say something."

"Remove my leg plate and wrap my leg, I am losing a lot of blood." Levi says as calmly as possible through his pained winces. He flops over on his back in the snow, letting out a sigh of pain as he looks towards the sky. He watches as the sun falls and dark clouds move in over the forest they have landed in from the northeast.

Estelle tries to calm herself but continues to panic while removing Levi's leg armor. Her hands are shaking from her nerves rather than the bone chilling wind atop the plateau. Her panic only grows when she pulls the armor from his leg, realizing the severity of the wound from the sword that pierced through his entire leg.

"Levi, you're... you are going to be alright. I will patch you up."

"Just wrap it up and put a tourniquet on my thigh then take care of yourself. If I stop breathing, just stay alive." Levi says as his head falls forward into the deep snow, and he fades out of consciousness.

Levi is taken into the void once again, where he was reunited with his father. He looks around the void, the torches are still blazing. Emanating a dim light but only to show more of the darkness, except for the blue torch that is flickering. He looks towards the blue torch. It suddenly becomes steady. The window of his father's eyes reappears as he walks closer, but he backs away, not wanting to relive the death of his father once again.

"Hello, my dear." A woman's voice says from behind him in the direction of one of the torches.

"Mother? Is that you?"

"Yes, Levi. Come here and talk to me."

Levi looks around the void noticing another torch has changed from a steady orange glow to a flickering blue flame. He walks towards the torch. As he closes the gap, a woman appears, in a blue velvet dress. Her hair is a soft brown color that flickers in the light of the torch.

"Mother..." Levi says as she embraces him with a loving hug.

"My son, I have missed you. Things were not easy when you left the Kingdom, I hope you are doing well."

"I will be alright, there is no need to worry about me. Wait a second, if you are here…"

"Yes, my time in Senary came to a close shortly after you left."

Levi lowers his head into his palms and begins to sob. "Mother…"

"Now, now. Do not blame yourself my little cub. Fate has a twisted way of rolling the dice sometimes."

Levi raises his head and looks his mother in her eyes. "Mother… who took your life…?"

"Hush now. Look through the window and watch as the dice roll in my last moments of life."

"I… I am afraid."

"The truth must be seen by your eyes, my son." She says holding her hand out for Levi to grasp while he watches.

Levi steps forward towards the window into the last moments of the woman he calls his mother's life. He takes her hand and her touch feels just as warm as it did the day, she took him in after his father passed. The window shows his mother's hands holding an old notebook and a quill. A vile half full of ink is sitting next to her on a wooden stand. A fire is crackling in the stone fireplace softly as she writes poetry in the old notebook. The door creaks open. She turns her head towards the sound with no hesitation. Through the door, her son, Theodore Ankore steps in. His head is hung down as if he has just been dragged through a gravel pit of sorrow.

"What is wrong, Theo?"

"Levi, mother. He has escaped."

"Oh, do not worry dear. I'm sure he will return with evidence to prove his innocence." She closes the notebook and places the quill in the vile of ink.

"He will return as a corpse, and he will die by my hand. I will not let this be a failure marked upon my name."

"Come now, your brother did nothing that he is being accused of. He is a sweet boy; he wouldn't hurt a fly."

"Enough! Stop defending that murderer! He is no brother to me!" Theodore throws his arms to his side, yelling at his mother.

"Theo. Calm down. He is your brother, and you are both my children."

Tears fall slowly down Theodore's face as he stares back at his mother.

"Why? Why mother?"

"Why what?"

"Why have you always favored him!? He is not your real son! You were ordered to take him in by the Queen, but you have always treated him as your favorite! Always!"

"Theo, please. I love both of you equally!"

"You are lying, you bitch! You hate me! You have hated me since the day that he came into this home! You treated me like I was second! Every accomplishment of mine was always overshadowed by something tedious he has done!"

"Theodore, I have given you all the love in the world a mother can give to her son. Your father, rest his soul, would turn in his grave to hear you speak this way."

"Father never would have allowed such disregard for one's own flesh and blood! Tell me why! Tell me why you've always treated him like he was the only one who mattered in your life!" Theodore demands, stomping towards his mother with ferocity and a green aura appearing around him. His mother pulls her hand towards her chest in disbelief over her son.

"I have treated you both equally. Why can you not see that?"

"Because it is not equal! He is a demon! Marked by God himself as the one who will bring ruin to the Kingdom! Yet you defend him and love him with all your heart! Why? Tell me why!" Theodore yells, pulling his mother to her feet by the collar of her velvet blue dress. She gasps for air as his tight grip voids her of breath.

"Please... Theodore... Listen to me..." She gasps for air.

"Enough!" Theodore yells, throwing her to the ground.

Theodore kneels overtop of her, wrapping his hands around her throat and squeezes the air from her body with a vise like grip.

"You have always loved him more!" Tears fall down his face as the green aura grows around him. "Why, mother? Why did you not love me the same! You are the reason for this! You should have shunned him away like the rest of the world! He is a demon!" Theodore's mother's face turns purple as her throat is being crushed by Theodore. She claws at his face. She is slapping and flailing her arms trying to break free from his grip. She takes her metal tipped quill that has fallen to the ground and thrusts it into the side of Theodore's face, sliding it down causing a large cut from his cheek to his eye. "You made me do this! This is your fault!" Theodore cries out as his mother's flailing comes to a stop. As her vision fades, the last image she sees is the face of her son bleeding, but his eyes are not filled with pain, but instead hatred, and jealousy.

The window fades to black. Levi steps backwards slowly. A black aura emanates from Levi's body as more of the void is absorbed into him. The blue and orange flames of the torches billow as the black mist of the void is drawn towards him. He lets out a yell of anger, pain, and sorrow. Holding his head as he yells.

Levi throws his arms to the side yelling upwards into the void as it wraps itself into his body. "I... will... kill him!"

"It appears it's time we depart my son. I will always love you. Remember that." His mother kisses him on the cheek as the void whips around him violently.

Before he gets a chance to speak, he awakes in the middle of the night. A soft campfire is flickering in a small shelter Estelle made from small trees and the cloak Levi was wearing. She is holding Levi tightly in her arms as he lay there awake watching the fire. Tears fell down his face. He takes his hand and places it over Estelle's softly trying not to wake her. He looks around the shelter. He notices his leg is bandaged and the bleeding has stopped, though the pain is still fully there. On the other side of the shelter he notices all the metal plate armor he and Estelle were wearing are laying in a pile and they are sitting on a woven blanket made of vines.

Estelle wrapped herself and Levi in the cloak he had

given her when they first met. He lies awake all

night. Marinating in his anguish. A black aura

emanates from his body as a wrath grows inside of

his mind for all who have wronged his loved ones.

He realizes the magical energy within him showing

itself around his body. He breathes in deeply.

Trying to calm his mind and not wake Estelle with

the immense pressure his aura is exuding in the

small shelter. As he slowly breathes, the aura fades

back into his body, and his mind becomes clear as if

he corked his emotions in a bottle and threw them

out to sea. Casting them away as if they never

existed.

The Northmen ready themselves within their

hand-built long hut atop of the mountain. They are

wrapping themselves in thick fur lined armor and

sharpening their axes happily with smiles across

each of their faces. Those who are ready to advance

are gathered near the doorway, cackling and singing a tune in their native language. Sweyn walks through the cloth doorway with a smile as large as can be spread across his face. As eager as his fellow Northmen to advance. Njal and Leif are behind him. Njal joins the gathering of men and women in song, while Leif looks around the room carefully, as if he is nervous of something.

"Listen, my brothers, and sisters. The Gods have graced us with a shield of snow to hide our entrance into that kingdom. Our King sent us to this foreign land over the mountains to deliver a simple message. As proud Northmen, we will deliver that with blades in our hands and smiles upon our faces. This Kingdom has expanded larger than any before. Our allies have warned our King of their 'triumphant' conquering of the great forest of Pirah. A sacred land belonging to our gods. The King wishes to send a warning. We will not fall. We will not retreat. We will not bow before a foreigner. We will slaughter their forces, steal their gold, pillage the entire Kingdom, and strike fear into the hearts of all who wish to conquer our homes. The time has come. May we feast together again in the afterlife, as family. Are you with me, my brothers, and sisters!?" Sweyn raises his axe into the air, yelling to his fellow Northmen.

Every warrior yells back with their battle cry. The feeling of excitement is synonymous with a cherished gathering of family.

"Remember! No one will return home until every person within that Kingdom has fallen before a Northmen's blade! The Gods be with us this day!" Sweyn yells, charging out of the cloth door.

The entire Northmen force charges behind him into battle. Down the mountain they storm. Running like children playing in a field, all happy and gallivanting towards what would seem certain death for all. The Northmen are trained warriors from birth. Their journey down the mountain is nothing more than a simple walk through a field to them. Each one's eyes locked on the Kingdom ahead of them, with the afterlife calling to them from the distance. Not a single tear is shed, only laughter and wide smiles are seen across each of their faces. Njal is running alongside Sweyn, though Leif is smiling as well. His smile is sullen. He looks towards the sun peeking through the white wall of snow just breaking the ocean's curve. He closes his eyes for a moment. A look of determination and hopefulness overcomes his dreary smile and his eyes become filled with a raging passion for battle as everyone running alongside him is sprinting towards their own graves with him.

The King of Triveria is pacing back and forth in his throne room. His mind filled with anxiety. His heart racing from the worry he feels within his mind.

"My King." A blue gemstone inlaid on a silver ring utters. It's Captain Ankore's voice.

"What do you need, Captain? Have you found Levi?"

"Yes, your highness. I need reinforcements. He has taken hold in Vorchid. Though the city is far too large for my forces to take."

"How do you know he's gone to Vorchid?" The King stops his pacing, he feels his heart begin to race even faster.

"I had an altercation with him, though he escaped using magic."

"He escaped!? How could you let this happen?"

"Sire, I will not fail again. Please send reinforcements. It's our only chance at taking him alive."

"Ankore, was the Amaranthine with him?" The king closes his eyes and tries to calm his racing heart.

"I believe so. An elven woman with amethyst hair was accompanying him. He took her along as he used a teleportation spell. Crowson has also betrayed the Kingdom and joined forces with Levi."

The King turns and looks out of his open glass door. Through the silence of the heavy snowfall, he hears laughter and the sound of screaming coming from the north. He steps outside. The strong wind nearly blows him off his feet. Through the snowfall, he sees an army of large, bearlike men and women attacking the Kingdom.

"Sire?"

"I cannot send you reinforcements! The Kingdom is under attack! Find Levi and the Amaranthine! If you do not contact me with news of their capture, then consider yourself dead!" The King yells into his ring, running into his throne room and to the hallway within the castle. "Men! Men! The Kingdom is under attack! Defend the north!" He runs down the hallway yelling orders to his subordinates.

The Northmen advance sporadically through the Kingdom. Slaughtering everyone in their path besides women without a weapon and children. They easily scale the north stone wall of the Kingdom. They are running through the streets in every direction, pillaging and destroying everything within their path. The two hundred northmen appear out of the white mist like birds of prey, hunting in the night. Screaming fills the streets as people of the Kingdom run from their homes. The forces within the Kingdom rush to the streets in formation. Their blades drawn and their leaders in the rear calling orders.

"Divide their forces! Light the flames!" Leif calls out to his fellow Northmen. Noticing the Knights are within large formation.

With vicious battle cries the Northmen run swiftly through the streets, distracting the Knights and breaking their formation easily. Groups of Knights disband after the multiple pillagers, only to be met with war axes and hammers around every corner. The Northmen mercilessly slaughter the Knights. As more Knights pour into the streets, more Northmen scale the wall as if their numbers will never cease.

"General! Call upon your forces! The Kingdom is under attack! Protect the Queen! Protect the princess! I will not let my Kingdom fall!" The King yells, desperately searching every room in the massive castle for his beloved wife and daughter. "Where are they!? Where are they!?" He slams open every door along the way.

"Father? What's going on?" The princess speaks from behind the King in a soft time. He turns and is greeted by a worried look on her face.

"Get to safety! The Kingdom is under attack! Where is your mother!?"

"I don't know father!? Who is attacking the Kingdom?"

"Find your mother and get to safety! I need to find the other members of the Six and make sure they're safe as well!"

"Father!" She yells as he runs down the hallway. She listens closely. Through the stampede of knights leaving the Castle, she hears screams and cries. Followed by the sound of boisterous laughter.

Within the abandoned storefront of Drixyl. The blood-stained floor and the broken shards of glass. Captain Ankore drives his fist deep into the hardwood wall in anger. He lets out a powerful yell.

"Fuck!" He yells pulling his unarmored hand, now full of splinters, from the wall.

"Captain. What is our plan?" Arthur asks in his monotone voice from behind the Captain.

"We must gather our forces, and advance on Vorchid. The Kingdom is under attack, we must retrieve Levi and the Amaranthine and return at once." Captain Ankore says, picking the splinters from his hand.

Arthur hands him a cloth to wrap his hand. "I will ready the platoon for our advance."

Ankore looks at Arthur with ferocity in his eyes. "We advance at dawn."

"Yes sir." Arthur turns and exits the storefront.

"This will soon come to an end. Do you hear me brother!? Do you hear me!?" Ankore yells in a fit of rage towards the ceiling of his commandeered home.

The sun rises over the forested region where Levi and Estelle lay in the cold. Their makeshift shelter only keeping the wind from them. Levi has kept the fire going with a pile of branches and sticks that Estelle gathered. Estelle is peacefully asleep, not willing to release her grip around Levi for even a moment. Levi reaches into the pouch on his side and feels around for the device Maria had given him, but only to find it has been broken into three pieces. He throws it from their shelter. Estelle's satchel is laying on the ground, he rummages

through it quietly searching for the one he gave her.
He pulls the cylindrical device from her satchel and
presses the silver button on it. Nothing happens. He
presses again, but only to watch it fail to operate. He
presses both buttons, the gold, and the silver one
multiple times. He throws it from the shelter into
the deep snow just outside. He lays his head back
on Estelle's chest, only to be comforted by her soft
breasts. He closes his eyes for a moment, then
quickly lifts his head again, realizing what he had
just done.

"Levi? Are you awake?"

"Yes. Thanks for patching me up."

"How long have you been awake?"

"Most of the night. I kept the fire going."

"I'm happy you are alright. Do you know
where we are by chance? I looked around while I
was gathering firewood, but I could not see
anything in the nighttime."

"I haven't a clue. I know we are in the general direction of Vorchid from Drixyl, but I was never very good at controlling the amount of energy I channel into spells. We could be one hundred miles away, or five. It all depends."

"I will go and look around since the sun's up. I will try to forage for food as well. Are you going to be alright here?"

"Yes. Give me a moment, I'll try to heal my leg a little that way I can walk."

"Just conserve your energy. I can handle it." She slides out from behind him and exits the shelter. "Why are the two things Maria gave us laying out here?"

"They did not work. So, I threw them."

"That is a little rude." Estelle chuckles. Levi shakes his head and unwraps the bandages around his wound.

The wound has turned black from the dry blood around it. The bandages are soaked completely in blood and his wound is nearing the point of infection already. Levi holds his hand over his wound and a blue aura appears around his hand. He closes his eyes and concentrates. The aura moves from his hand onto the wound, and it begins to close slowly. He winces in pain as his bone is forming back together. He lets out a verbal yell as the wound slowly closes into a thick scar. Though his bone has fused back together, and his skin has sealed. The ligaments and muscles could not heal within the time Levi was able to control his magical energy.

Estelle is running through the forest, diligently picking snowberries and different plants for them to eat. Amid her distracted mind, she feels as though she is being watched. She stands and peers around the open forest slowly.

"Is someone there?" She says to the empty forest, that only replies with a faint gust of wind. "I must be going crazy from all of this stress." She says to herself with a sigh.

From the treetops, a set of hungry eyes watches Estelle begin her walk back towards the shelter. The eyes gaze at her with a bloodlust of a starving animal. The beast has wrapped itself in the treetops. Its body engulfing nearly eight trees. Its large serpentine body is suspended by its long razer like claws digging into the trunk of two trees while hiding its large winged arms within the desolate snow-covered crowns. As Estelle takes each step, the beast slowly serpentines through the treetops, stalking its prey as skillful as a master assassin.

Estelle notices a thick block of snow fall from the treetops. Already in a nervous state. She turns around rapidly and looks towards the sky. The moment her eyes gaze into the trees, she is in shock.

"A wyvern..." She whispers to herself.

Estelle drops what little food she has gathered in the deep snow and sprints towards the shelter. The wyvern drops to the ground. Graceful. Menacing. Snow falls from the trees as if an earthquake has just shaken the world's core. The wyvern's pursuit begins.

Estelle rushes towards the shelter. She feels the powerful stomps of the gigantic wyvern quickly approaching her. The adrenaline she feels is fueling her body. The only thought in her mind. Protect Levi.

"Levi! We must go now. Please there's a wyvern in the forest and it's coming!" Estelle dives into the shelter in a panic.

"A wyvern? They've been extinct for nearly one hundred years." Levi tries to calm her down.

"Levi, now!" She pulls Levi to a stand. The ground shakes as if its trees were falling just behind the shelter. Levi winces in pain as the weight of his body presses on his injured leg. "Come on. We have to go!" Estelle wraps Levi's arm around her shoulder and leaves the shelter with Levi hobbling next to her as quickly as he can.

An ear-piercing screech stuns them both. Estelle lowers her head, trying to cover her sensitive ears. Levi turns and draws his sword the dwarven man in Drixyl gave to him. The runes engraved on the blade of his sword glow with a fiery red glow as Levi channels what magic he can muster into them. Estelle opens her eyes just a small way. Seeing Levi draw his sword. Before she can get a word out to Levi. His hand presses on her arm. The blue light that saved them from the Captain Ankore's men in Drixyl suddenly flashes before her eyes.

Estelle falls to the ground a short way in the deep powdery snow. She tumbles and rolls until she comes to a stop. She quickly pokes her head up and looks around.

"Levi!? Levi!" She yells coming to a stand in an immense panic.

"Estelle? Estelle is that you?!" Kristoff's voice says from a distance.

"Kristoff!?" She yells back.

Kristoff quickly rides to her aid on top of his commandeered horse. Jumping from the horse as it slows and looking her up and down for any injuries.

"Estelle, where's Levi!?" He asks with a deep concern in his voice.

"I do not know!? He teleported us away from a Wyvern, but he did not land with me!?"

"Estelle, was he still injured?"

"Yes, but he was able to stand." Estelle tries to calm herself down.

"He must have healed himself. If you are here and he is not, then he only teleported you to safety. He must have been nearly out of magical energy."

"Kristoff, we have to help him!"

"Where were you last!?"

"On top of a forested plateau."

"Come on!" Kristoff says jumping onto his horse and extending his hand to Estelle.

She takes hold of his hand and leaps onto the horse behind him. Kristoff cracks the reins of the horse and quickly up the hill they rise towards the forest. Estelle realizes that Levi was not able to teleport her far away. As they trot towards the plateaus caprock, the sound of the Wyvern's screech and Levi's yells ring through their ears as if they are stuck in a nightmare.

With each step their horse takes. Estelle feels her heart continue to beat faster. The sound of the screeches and yells are muffled by her panic. Time seems to be nearing a halt as she fears the worst. Suddenly Kristoff pulls the horse to a complete stop. Estelle looks forward to seeing Levi standing above the slain body of the Wyvern. His sword is driven deep into the skull of the massive Wyvern. As the red glow that once engulfed his blade now fades into the air like nothing. Levi is holding himself up with just his hands on his blade. Blood is dripping from his body. The snow is absorbing the scarlet essence of Levi's life as it pools at his feet.

Estelle and Kristoff run to his side, praying that he is still breathing. As Estelle places her hand on his back. Her eyes are scarred with the sight of Levi's shredded torso from the Wyvern's talons. The deep claws cut completely through his armor and into his flesh. She gasps as he lets out a deep breath. The steam drifts through the air as if his soul has left his body. Levi falls backwards into the snow with Estelle and Kristoff kneeling next to him. He looks to the bright blue sky as his vision is encumbered with a void once again.

Chapter 8: The Eternal Blossom

The sun rises above Drixyl the next day. Captain Ankore is pacing back and forth in front of his platoon of knights just outside of the northern gate of Drixyl. Arthur and Mattaeus are sitting atop their loyal steeds awaiting orders from their Captain. The platoon of knights stands at the ready to advance, though their spirits do not radiate the same morale as they once did before.

"Men. It is imperative that we complete our mission at once. Our Kingdom… no, our homes are under attack. Our families are defenseless within Triveria's once impenetrable walls of stone. Reinforcements will not be coming to our aid. We must take the city of Vorchid by force. Our numbers are few. Theirs are great. Though our prowess in battle vastly outweighs whatever rabble they have defending their streets. I once said that we are required to bring Levi and the Amaranthine back alive. Though for the sake of our Kingdom's name and the safety of our families, if the opportunity arises, and all else fails, you have my permission as field commander to take their lives. We believe the Amaranthine to be the elven woman who Levi brought with him as a prisoner to Drixyl in their attempt to take my life. Be warned, Levi is a profound swordsman. I am not aware of what allies he may have gathered either. Be prepared for the worse. Alright. That is all. Move out." Captain Ankore says with a sullen ferocity in his voice.

He places his helmet over his head and mounts his horse next to Arthur and Mattaeus, beginning their journey towards Vorchid as a platoon. Though their numbers are weak, each Knight of Triveria is a well-trained warrior capable of defeating any commoner in a game of blades. Their horses stampede down the snow beaten path.

The rumble of their hooves is synonymous with an earthquake that would shake an entire village to the ground. Each soldier ready to return home from their long journey.

The bustling streets of Vorchid are wrought with a distinct smell. The smell of spoiled meat and decaying vegetables. The merchant's goods are no longer appealing to their customers. As each day passes, more and more of those living within Vorchid are refusing to buy goods. Most have taken to traveling to the nearby village of Levenwood. Where farmlands are bountiful and there is food o' plenty.

Within the small brick and mortar building Maria calls her home, a ruckus has sparked within. From the streets, only a few passersby stop and gawk through the windows as broken glass and yelling has drawn their attention.

Maria and Estelle are yelling at one another, bickering over Levi's well-being, while Kristoff sits quietly next to Levi as he lays unconscious on the sofa. Bandages are wrapped around Levi's body and limbs, though none appear to be bloody. Kristoff shakes his head at Estelle and Maria, who are quarrelling like two old women shopping in the same store for the same item.

"Do you see this Levi? This is what you cause." Kristoff looks towards Levi. "Oh, I see how it is. Just ignore me." He chuckles. "It is fine, you can take your little nap while I sit here and listen to these two yell at one another."

Levi's unconscious mind is taken deep into the void where he was reunited with his loved ones. He walks slowly through the black misty void. Each footstep echoes as if he were in an opera hall. He looks around and can see the two torches flickering blue, and the rest steadily burning with an orange flame. He approaches the orange flames, though none change to the flickering blue light.

"Father? Mother?" He says into the echoing void. But only hears his voice again, and again. "What is this place? I do not understand why I keep being brought here." He says with a limp confused tone. He walks towards the flickering blue flame where his father stood. The void opens into the same window to his father's eyes. He backs away quickly, afraid to relive the last moments of his father's life once again.

"I do not understand!" He yells into the void, flailing around wildly. "Why am I here!? Why am I being shown these tragedies! Why! Why must I relive this! Why must I suffer through their pain!?" He yells.

"To become who you truly are. Levi." A woman's voice says from behind him. He turns around quickly.

"Who is it?" He says walking towards the voice.

"We've never met before. Though I have watched over you, your entire life." The voice says from the void.

"Who… who are you?" Levi stops and stares into the direction of the voice just past the glowing orange torches.

"I am your mother. The mother that gave you life."

"My real mother…?" Levi feels an overwhelming feeling of guilt overshadow his mind. "Why can I not see you?" He asks in desperation.

"This place is within your mind. Those within it can only appear as you know them. We have never met sadly. I cannot manifest within this place because of the lack of memory of my appearance."

"How are you here, mother?" Levi investigates the void's call.

"Each person within this place is connected to you. They have given you fragments of their energy throughout their life, or in my case I gave you everything I had left within my body. A piece of their soul lives within you." The voice says, though it is as if the voice is right in front of Levi.

"Does that mean that each of these torches are pieces of someone's soul?" He looks around at all the torches.

"Yes, they will continue to grow as your life goes on. It appears you have already spoken to two of them."

"But all I've been shown is the remaining moments of their life... I do not understand."

"Each sliver of the souls living within your mind has shared their last moments with you, though it's not necessarily easy to watch. Each of these torches must turn blue for you to become what the Gods have destined you to be." The voice says into his ear.

"What do you mean? What am I…?" He asks, standing motionless in the void.

"You are the one who must stop the cycle."

"Stop the cycle…?"

"Time will show the answers to your questions. For now, return to your body. I will guide you along the path through the torches whenever you wish to return here. Goodbye, my son. I'll be waiting for you."

"Mother!? How can I return here!?" Levi shouts as he wakes sitting up rapidly yelling into the room full of bickering.

"Levi!" Estelle leaps towards Levi, knocking him back over out of excitement.

"Estelle? Are you alright? Did you get hurt?"

"No! I am fine. But are you alright? Yovanna and Maria healed you the best they could, but you were nearly dead!" Estelle grabs his face and looks him over.

"I'm fine. Where are we?" Levi looks around, being greeted with his peers astonished looks that he has just woken up as if he were taking a nap.

"Levi, is your mind doing alright? You've just yelled about your mother upon your awakening…" Kristoff asks curiously, placing his hand on Levi's shoulder.

"Just a dream is all." Levi says looking at Maria. "Thank you for healing my wounds." He nods at Yovanna as well.

"Levi, I am sorry I've betrayed you. You as well, Estelle." Yovanna raises her head and says mournfully.

"It is fine. Nothing I'm not used to." Levi says with a grin.

"Yovanna, I want to accept that apology. But Levi and I were almost killed because of you. I cannot forgive you." Estelle crosses her arms and looks away from the girl she once called a friend.

Yovanna lowers her head. "I understand, Estelle."

"Well, I guess now would be the best time to say this. I am turning myself in. I will return to the Kingdom with Theodore." Levi says solemnly as he peers around the room at shocked faces.

Maria flails her arms in disbelief. "Levi, you cannot be serious. You are going to be killed instantly!"

"No, only if I resist. When that knight stabbed through my leg, he was not aiming to kill me. He purposely missed the artery. If he were intending to kill me, he would have done so." Levi stands, still in pain though minor at that.

"If you are going… then I am going too." Estelle says with hesitant determination in her voice.

"No, they are only looking for me. It is best that you stay."

"They are after both of you." Yovanna says with a sigh to the ignorance of the group's knowledge of the knight's objectives.

Levi turns his head quickly in shock. "What? Why are they after Estelle?"

"Theodore has been referring to someone as something called the Amaranthine. I don't know what it means, but the King ordered him to bring both of you back to the Kingdom alive." Yovanna says calmly.

"The Amaranthine…" Maria says quietly to herself, thinking. She steps out of the room quickly. She walks down the hall into her study and quickly looks through the large bookshelves. She pulls an old book from the shelf and flips through the yellowed pages. Silently she reads the open page and walks back to the room full of her peers. "I know I've seen it somewhere. The Amaranthine is a woman who guides the Wolf through the darkness." She reads from the book.

"Guides the Wolf through the darkness?" Estelle asks curiously.

"To put it simple. The Sacred Six hold the weight of the cardinal sins of the world. Though there are only six, each one is marked with a different animal, representing their sin. For instance, I was born with the raven upon my neck." Maria lowers her collar and reveals a black Raven just above her shoulder blade.

"I was born with the wolf." Levi unwraps the bandages around his upper arm and reveals a wolf's head howling.

"What do they represent?" Estelle asks curiously, feeling the mark on Levi's arm.

"Mine represents lust. Levi's represents wrath."

"Do they reflect on personalities?" Yovanna asks curiously.

"They have strong impacts on the person's life. I tend to find myself lusting far more than a normal woman. Sometimes it's uncontrollable." Maria answers openly.

"What about you, Levi?"

"I have had no signs of it impacting my personality. It is just a birthmark. Nothing more."

"You always have been calm and level headed." Kristoff says looking towards Levi.

Maria extends her hand and places it on top of Levi's head. A white aura appears on her hand as she closes her eyes. Suddenly she lets go and steps backwards quickly. As if she has been frightened by something.

"Maria, what was that?" Kristoff asks with a chuckle.

"I... I do not know. I just felt... something." She says trying to control her breathing to calm down.

"May I?" Yovanna asks Levi.

"Go ahead." Levi says while looking at Maria.

Yovanna extends her hand; a soft white aura appears on her hand as he eyes close. Her mind is filled with a darkness, one only that of a demon would bring upon the mind of the world. She winces but delves further. Into the void of Levi's mind. She sees death, and destruction, some from times past and many from times ahead.

Everyone in the room is watching Yovanna intently. Tears begin to slowly run down her face as she winces, though she still focuses her aura on Levi. Levi is staring at Maria still, who is unable to calm her mind.

Suddenly Yovanna's breathing becomes a struggle. The tears flow like a river as she lets out a painful cry. Levi's eyes are locked forward, as if he is trying to control whatever is roaming within his mind. Yovanna releases her aura and falls backward nearly losing consciousness, though Kristoff catches her just before she hits the ground. Levi shakes his head and begins breathing heavy.

"Never do that...again." Levi says, trying to catch his breath.

"Levi. I saw everything..." Yovanna says holding onto Kristoff as she tries to stand. "Everything in your life, every tragedy, every loss, every death. Everything you have done... You have just let them culminate in your mind. You have been keeping them locked deep away in your mind..." Yovanna says looking at Levi both concerned and terrified.

"If I am known as the Amaranthine, then I want to try that. How do I do it?" Estelle asks Maria.

"Levi, are you alright if she tries?"

"I would prefer if she didn't."

"Oh, come on. Clearly we are meant to meet so I have to try something!" Estelle stomps.

Levi looks towards Estelle and shakes his head. "Fine."

"Okay Estelle, place your hand on Levi's head. Channel your magic into his mind. Visualize yourself inside Levi's head, inside of his consciousness."

"Okay." Estelle nods and places her hands-on Levi's head.

Estelle closes her eyes and visualizes herself inside of Levi's mind. Instantly she is placed into the void where the torches are flickering dimly.

"Where am I?" She says aloud in the void.

"You are in my mind." Levi says standing next to her.

Estelle looks around for a moment. "What was the big deal that those two were panicking about? It is just dark, and there are just torches.... Wait are these the torches you saw in Kreitor?"

"Yes. These are the torches. Each one represents someone that I am connected to in some way or another. The two that are flickering blue I have already met and seen their fate. The first was my father, and the second was my adoptive mother."

"Seen their fate?"

"Who killed them, and the last moments of their life."

"Levi…"

Levi looks into Estelle's beautiful amethyst eyes. "What the others saw was not this. I am not entirely sure what they saw, but it was not my consciousness. Normally while I am in here, I meet someone, but it has only been whenever I've been unconscious."

"I see you have found her." The voice of Levi's birth mother echoes from the depths of the void.

Estelle looks around, trying to find the voice. "Levi, who is that?"

"That is my mother. My real mother."

"It is a pleasure to meet you, though not technically. If you are in here, and he is in here while still conscious then you must be the Amaranthine."

"That is what everyone is saying I am, but what does it mean?" Estelle asks curiously, looking upwards.

"It means you are the flower that soothes the Wolf, you are the pathway through the darkness of Levi's mind."

"The darkness?"

"Yes, this black void as you see it. This is Levi's magical energy; this is the weight he bears for the world. With each outburst of emotion, this energy is moved from his mind and into his body. It is dangerous, destructive, fatal even. If this energy were to be released without control, then the world would surely be in ruin."

"I do not understand this. Why me, why am I the one who must bear this weight?" Levi shouts into the void as it begins to whip around him.

"Calm down, my son. You bear the sin of Wrath. This energy is released through anger. Though I have watched over you, I know that you have not been able to hold it back. It is powerful. Far more powerful than your mind."

"How can I help Levi?" Estelle asks.

"You must venture with him through the void. Decipher the message that the torches hold. Build the pathway towards salvation. Overcome the asperity the journey will bring and rebuild this rotten world on the brink of destruction. I must warn you both, the path ahead is only going to get worse. You have lost an Amaranthine once Levi, you must not lose her again." Levi's mother says from the void as it fades.

"It seems we're in this for the long haul."
Levi says to Estelle.

"I told you once that I'm going where you go.
At least I have some sort of explanation as to why I
desire to be by your side. But Levi, what did she
mean that you have lost an Amaranthine?"

"Yes, it seems my growing feelings are more
than natural. To answer your question Estelle, I am
not entirely sure. The feelings I have towards you
and the sense of being drawn to you is like what I
felt with Amelia." Levi says closing his eyes for a
moment.

"Who is Amelia?" Estelle asks curiously.

"She was someone… special to me. She was
killed by my brother in the Kingdom in front of my
eyes because of my sins. I will never forgive myself
for that, and I know I must atone for my failures."

"Was she a past love?"

"Do you remember how I looked at you
when we were on the mountains above Drixyl?"

"Yes. I remember you would not take your eyes off me."

"You look identical to her, except for pointier ears. Your eyes breathe a certain warmth into me, a radiance of light through the darkness of my mind. It was the same feeling I felt with her when I fell in love with her."

"Are you saying you are in love with me?" Estelle blushes happily.

"I do not know, but I know that I will do anything to keep you safe, Estelle." Levi says, wrapping one arm around her shoulders.

Estelle turns and hugs Levi tightly around his waist. "I knew there was some reason we met. When this is all over maybe we can find a quiet place to adventure rather than these dreadful cold mountains." Estelle chuckles.

"Maybe we can." Levi laughs. "Are you ready to return to the real world now, were your questions answered?"

"Hmm." Estelle holds her hand to her chin. "I guess, for now." She chuckles.

Suddenly Estelle opens her eyes and a wide smile sprawls across her face. Levi's eyes open and he is greeted with her vibrant amethyst eyes, giving his body a warming feeling. In the room there is immense commotion as the two have a heartfelt moment.

"Estelle, Levi!? Are you two alright?" Maria asks hastily.

"I am fine." Levi stands and walks out of the room.

"Maria, if he loses control of his emotions. The outburst of magical energy within him will destroy everything around him. But if he keeps holding everything back. He is likely to lose his own life from the amount of energy." Kristoff helps Yovanna sit down next to him on the luxurious sofa.

"How far did you go? I could not get past the void. It was like my energy was being devoured by… by something. I do not even know how to describe it."

"I felt it eating away at my energy. In legend, the Wolf is known as a demon. That might be why. I am afraid if he endures one more loss in his life, all of his energy will be released." Yovanna lays her head back on the comfortable sofa, closing her eyes as she tries to ease the pain she felt from venturing into Levi's mind.

"He will be okay." Estelle smiles.

The four look out the doorway in the hall, seeing Levi pass by stomping. Fully armored with his horns on his helmet towering above him and sheathing his sword on his back.

"Where are you going?" Kristoff stands and asks.

"Out." Levi opens the door and slams it shut behind him.

"What's gotten into him?" Kristoff asks the group.

"Who knows. He has always been like that." Maria says shaking her head.

"Estelle, what did you see. You did not seem to have any trouble." Kristoff asks with curiosity.

"I was inside of his mind. I met his mother, and he and I talked to her. I understand a lot of things now. She explained what she could." Estelle smiles.

"You were in his mind? Did you encounter the void?"

"We were inside of it. The void is his pent-up emotion, the weight he bears for the world."

"Perhaps, you are the Amaranthine." Maria nods as she begins to think of Estelle's words.

"Oh, before I forget, Maria, your device things are on top of that plateau still. Levi threw them out because his broke and mine didn't work."

"Right, about that..." Maria pauses. "Yours was a fake."

"Excuse me?"

"It was not real. Well it was a real transporter. But I did not link it to this location like I did the other two."

"What? Why?"

"I thought…"

"She thought you were also with the Triverian army with blondie over here." Kristoff snarls walking out of the room.

"You thought I was against you!? Against Levi!" Estelle yells.

"I was not entirely sure. The plan was to leave you and her in Drixyl. She would still be there, but Kristoff insisted on bringing her back."

"What is wrong with you!?" Estelle pushes Maria in anger.

"Calm down! Things turned out alright!"

"Because Levi almost died! Twice! Are you kidding me!?" Estelle grabs Maria by her collar angrily.

"Estelle, we do not need to do this. It will not end well for you." Maria says, grabbing Estelle's wrists tightly.

"Oh, calm yourselves. It is not the first time that idiots almost died. Highly unlikely to be that last either." Kristoff chuckles, trying to ease the tense situation.

"I am going after Levi. I refuse to be in the same room as that woman!" Estelle takes her cloak and leaves Maria's home. Slamming the door behind her.

"My, she is perfect for him." Kristoff chuckles as he sits down next to Yovanna.

"Shut up, Kristoff. I do not want to hear another word about her." Maria says with a jealous tone of voice.

"Estelle really likes Levi. She has not stopped talking about him since he saved us from the yetari's in the mountains of Drixyl." Yovanna says, looking at Maria.

"Kristoff, I'm going out. Make sure she does not go anywhere. If she does, please kill her. I still do not like the idea of her being here." Maria pulls on a black fur coat and leaves her home.

"Will do." Kristoff says looking at Yovanna with a smile.

"I am sorry about everything, Kristoff. Most of this mess is caused by me."

"No need to apologize to me. We would have found Levi one way or another, you just sped up the process. Besides, I am sure Levi is not all that concerned about it anyway. He never was the type to hold grudges."

"I do not think you really understand Levi."

"What? I have known him my whole life. He is my best friend."

"When I was inside of his mind. I saw terrible things, anger, almost demon like power being reserved within him. I saw flashes of things he has done. People he has killed and slaughtered. He is not showing how he really sees the world."

"I see. Perhaps I ought to have a talk with him. Anyways, I should probably go find Levi. Who knows what sort of trouble he will get himself into?" He continues. "Care to come along?" Kristoff says, wrapping a scarf around his neck and strapping the piece of armor embedded with a Triverian stone shard on his arm.

"I would be happy to help. It is the least I can do."

"Come along then." Kristoff leads the way out the door promptly.

Maria knocks on the door of Isabella's estate angrily. No answer. She knocks again, but harder.

She hears footsteps running down the stairs towards the door.

"Give me a moment!" Bella says from behind the door. She swings it open. Revealing that she is wearing nothing, but a towel wrapped around her chest. Her soaking wet hair draped over her shoulders. Maria feels an uncontrollable urge overcome her body. She grabs Isabella by the back of her neck and kisses her deeply. They share a long kiss. Maria pulls away, and without hesitation. Bella pulls her in and closes the door behind them quickly.

Through the streets of Vorchid, Estelle runs, frantically searching for Levi. She scours the top of the crowds from the street sides. Desperately hoping to catch but a glimpse of the two black horns upon Levi's helm. No sign of him anywhere. She runs down the street side through the crowds. Narrowly avoiding wagons and horses as they pass by.

"Levi!" She calls out for him, but her beckoning is drowned out by the chatter of the busy streets.

Kristoff and Yovanna are not far behind her. Kristoff hears her call out and pushes through the crowds to catch up to her holding Yovanna's hand so as not to lose her. Suddenly the black plate of armor he still has on his arm glows dimly from the blue shard of sapphire.

"Captain, we have reached the outskirts of the city. Shall we move in?"

"No, set up camp in the forest outside. We will be attacking in the night to take over the town."

"As you wish."

"This is not good." Kristoff listens carefully to the voices speaking from the gemstone. "I have to find Levi, now. Estelle! Wait up! Estelle!" He yells running faster through the streets.

"Kristoff, was that Ankore?"

"Yes. We must hurry."

Estelle turns around instantly. She sees Kristoff quickly pushing through the crowds towards her. In just a moment, he nimbly greets her with desperation marked on his face.

"We have to find Levi immediately! The platoon of Knights is going to attack Vorchid in the night!" Kristoff says.

"What? They are going to attack an entire city. That is ridiculous." She scoffed at Kristoff's statement.

"Estelle, these men are the most ruthless warriors the kingdom has to offer. These guards will not stand a chance against the knights. No matter how many there are."

"Fine, I believe you. It might be best if one of us warns Isabella."

"You're right. I will go to her estate. Hopefully, she is home."

"I'm going to keep looking for Levi. I do not like when he wanders off alone. It makes me feel uneasy."

"Come to the estate when you find him. We will regroup and meet up there."

"Okay. Levi!" She yells out, continuing down the street quickly.

"Is this alright? I'm not being to forward, am I?" Kristoff says, taking Yovanna's hand once again.

"No, I do not mind. It is comforting in fact." Yovanna smiles kindly at Kristoff.

"Wonderful. Let us continue." Kristoff says walking with her down the street quickly towards the estate of Isabella Ryker.

As they approach, Kristoff notices the door is not fully shut. His stomach sinks. His mind takes a turn towards the dark path as he wonders what could have come of the Lord of Vorchid, and why she would leave her door open. He creeps up to it. He gently pushes the door open with his free hand while holding Yovanna tightly in the other. As he opens the door, he notices Maria's fur coat is laying on the floor. He begins to panic just a little. He peeks his head in and looks down the long marble floored hallway, noticing a wet towel laying on the floor as well. He raises his eyebrow in curiosity. He and Yovanna step into the estate and notice a trail of clothing has been dropped in a line down the hallway into a room.

"Um, pardon the intrusion is anyone home!?" He yells into the large estate.

"Just a minute!" Isabella says from the room where the clothing leads.

"Perhaps she had fallen in the snow." Kristoff says nervously as he looks at Yovanna.

"That explains it." Yovanna retorts with a sarcastic tone and smile.

Isabella comes from around the corner wrapped in a long trench coat. Her legs and upper chest exposed, signifying she is wearing nothing underneath. She is panting a little, and her face is completely red.

"Pardon the... interruption, miss Isabella. But the platoon of Triverian Knights is planning to attack the city tonight."

"What!? How many are they!? Are they well-armed!? Where are they attacking from!?"

"Oh my, fifty or so, yes, and unknown."

"I must call upon my guards to defend the city. I cannot allow my city to be attacked, we've already suffered a heavy economic loss from the lack of commerce." Isabella says in a panic. The unbuttoned trench coat slips open revealing a glimpse at her unclothed body underneath. Kristoff looks away, trying not to be rude. Yovanna stares at Isabella blankly.

"Miss, I do not mean to be rude but your coat. It is slipping."

"Oh dear." Bella covers herself once again.

"By chance, is Maria here?"

"No, I am here alone."

"I see. So that is not Maria's coat?" Kristoff points at the fur coat on the ground.

"Oh my! No, that is mine! I fell in the snow!"

"Uh huh. Okay, whatever you say." Yovanna says smugly.

"Alright, we will be leaving then. Make sure your guards are ready." Kristoff says, taking Yovanna by the hand once again and walking back out the door.

"Are they gone!?" Maria peeks her head from around the corner.

"Yes, I am sorry to cut our fun short. The Triverian knights are planning to attack the city tonight. I need to prepare with the guards."

"Oh lord, this is not good." Maria runs out from the room completely nude picking up her dropped clothing.

Estelle is steadily making her way down the street; she notices Levi's black horns towering above the crowd in the distance. He ducks his head and enters the blacksmith shop where they have previously met the dwarven blacksmith. She pushes through the crowds. Knocking a few people over along the way. She storms into the blacksmith's shop and anger overtakes her normally pleasant smile.

"Levi! You are an idiot!" She yells at him, interrupting the conversation between him and the blacksmith.

"Seems you have gone and made the princess a little angry with you. It's not wise to make a woman upset, young man." The dwarf chuckles boisterously.

"I am not sure what I did." Levi turns around and looks at Estelle.

"Why did you leave!? I told you before when you go somewhere just take me along! It is not safe leaving alone!" Estelle stomps towards Levi.

"I needed to step out. The commotion would have given me a headache. I can handle myself though."

"Last time I let you handle something yourself, you almost got yourself killed! Never again!" A few tears begin to fall down her face. She balls her fist and taps Levi's chest armor. Laying her head as she cries on his chest. "Levi, I don't want to lose you. I don't want to lose the only person that means anything to me in my life!" Estelle cries out.

"Seems like he has really won her heart. Aye, best the princess gives her heart to someone she wishes instead of that daft elven boy the King chose for her." The blacksmith thinks to himself with a smile.

"Estelle, I am sorry. When Yovanna was in my head. It was like I had to hold back a demon from coming from the gates of hell. I had to leave.

As soon as you left my mind, I almost lost myself. I do not know why."

"Are you feeling better now?" She raises her head and looks at him through teary eyes.

"Yes. Better now that I am with you, actually." He wipes the tears from her face and hugs her tightly.

"Awe isn't that sweet." The dwarven blacksmith says with a playful chuckle.

"Lok, it is best if you leave town immediately. Go to Levenwood or hide away in the mountains for a while. The Triverian Knights are going to destroy the city in the night." Levi says turning his head while still hugging Estelle.

"What!? I will not leave my store. They can have it over my dead body!" He says angrily.

"Levi, I was going to tell you that. How did you know?"

"I saw two members of the Fourth Edict outside of town while I was walking. Then I heard Ankore speak to them through this gauntlet." Levi holds the gauntlet in the air.

"What are you going to do?" Estelle asks with worry in her voice.

"I don't know yet. Lok, can you embed these stones in my gauntlet."

"Sure thing. Give it here." He holds his hand out.

Levi unstraps his gauntlet and slides it from his arm, handing Lok the gauntlet of the fourth Edict armor and his own. The dwarven blacksmith takes them back to his forge and gets to work steadily.

"We are to meet Kristoff and Yovanna at Isabella's estate after I found you. We can go there right after we're done here."

"Alright." Levi nods in agreeance.

"Levi, I can't let you turn yourself in. They are just going to kill us both when we get to the kingdom. We have to fight."

"No. This is not your fight. It is mine. I have a debt to collect with Ankore, and the King." Levi says looking down into Estelle's eyes.

"Can we just run? Far away from here. Just please..." She sobs.

"I cannot run any longer. The time's come for me to face reality for what it is."

"After this is done, can we go on adventures together? Just live our lives happily?" Estelle pleas.

"Estelle. I cannot promise I'll live through tonight."

"Stop it! Stop saying that!" She begins to cry again.

"Here you are. Nice and polished for you. Mind if I keep this black gauntlet. Its craftsmanship is exquisite. I'd like to study it." Lok hands Levi his gauntlet back.

"You're more than welcome to it." Levi takes his gauntlet and places it back over his hand. "How much do I owe you?"

"Not a thing. Just promise me, you will keep her safe. I'd hate to see the princess fall to a couple of insignificant bugs like the knights of Triveria." He says with a smile.

"She'll be safe. I promise."

"Yourself as well, I cannot have her come back crying in my shop. Turns away a lot of customers." He chuckles.

"I'll do my best." Levi says.

The Triverian knights arrive in the forest just east of Vorchid as the sun sets across the snow-covered land. Arthur and Mattaeus have set up makeshift camp using downed trees and blankets that covered their horses. A fire is raging in the center with food being cooked overtop of it. Captain Ankore dismounts his steed and joins them by the fire.

"How many guards did you see?" He asks immediately.

"Not many. Perhaps fifteen, twenty."

"This will be easier than I thought. Perhaps I was too hasty in requesting reinforcements. No matter, by sunrise, victory will be ours, and we will be returning home by the afternoon."

"Hungry, Captain?"

"Very." Captain Ankore joins Arthur and Mattaeus by the fire. Arthur hands Ankore a slab of meat on a clean knife. "Thank you."

"Captain. I'm worried about my family in the kingdom."

"Aye. We all are. Whoever attacked the kingdom... they will meet the end of our blades. We will slaughter all of them." Ankore takes a large bite from the slab of meat as the rest of the platoon arrives in the forest.

"Have you heard anything else from the King?"

"No, I will contact him soon. I am sure he has barricaded himself within the walls of his castle with the other members of the six and his family."

"Right…" Arthur says solemnly, thinking of the safety of his family. "I have a daughter. She just turned three a day before we departed the kingdom. I hope I can see her smiling face when I return. I don't know if I could live on… knowing she'd been hurt in my absence." Arthur says softly as tears drip from his helmet.

"She'll be alright. Your wife is a warrior herself; you know." Mattaeus says happily, trying to cheer up Arthur and ease his mind.

"It's not right that I'm not there. I can't stop thinking of their safety."

"Use that when we encounter Levi this evening. Fight with ferocity. Do not do it for the Kingdom, do it for your family. The faster we capture or kill Levi, the faster we can depart this barren land for the Kingdom."

"I will, Captain." Arthur says sobbing inside of his helm.

Chapter 9: As the Flower Wilts

The Kingdom of Triveria is steadily enduring the attack of the Northmen. Their forces, though great in number, are being slaughtered by the unorthodox fighting style of the Northmen. A seemingly endless flow of knight's stomp through the raging fires and river of blood running through the streets of the Kingdom. The Northmen are savages of war compared to the formation bound knights. Divide and conquer. A simple strategy. Though immensely effective against large formations of soldiers under the command of one. For each slain foreigner to the Kingdom, lay twenty armored knights below their body. Each Northmen still bare their wide smile across their blood soaked faces. The battle rages on. The Northmen continue to pillage the homes and stores of the Kingdom.

Ransacked, demolished and stained in blood. The

Kingdom looks as though it is a sacrifice to the

God's from the Northmen's homeland.

Inside the seemingly impenetrable walls of

the King's castle. A panic strikes through the King.

He cannot find his Queen and has barricaded

himself in the chamber where the council holds

their meetings. With him are the council members

and the two members of the Sacred Six that remain

in the kingdom. His daughter the princess, and

Amelia Van Lryia. They sit around the table where

the stone map of Senary is etched into the stone. The

King has begun to lose his temper, while his

daughter, frightened by the attack huddles next to

him closely. Amelia is pacing back and forth around

the room itching to join the battle.

"Your highness. This is ridiculous! We are

the members of the Sacred Six. Chosen at birth to

save the Kingdom from its downfall! Why are we

forced to hide like children!" Olivia yells at the King angrily.

The King slams his hand on the stone table. "Olivia. I cannot risk losing you in the battle. It is imperative that you stay safe for the Kingdom."

"I will not hide! I am a warrior!" She yells.

"Let her go. She may be able to turn the tide of this battle." A council member says from across the table.

"I will not!" The King yells.

"The Kingdom is falling, your highness." The same council member stands and looks out of the window.

The King stands from his seat and walks towards the window. His shadowed face is illuminated from the raging fire spreading from building to building. The small fires the Northmen set are now a raging inferno that has spread throughout the wooden homesteads throughout the kingdom. From the window high above the castle.

Njal, covered in blood and with a limp arm, is battling a platoon of knights alone. As each one attacks, he overpowers them with brute force, and ends their life with his axe in the next motion.

"This… is absurd. One man is fighting an entire platoon…" The king says in shock, backing away from the window. The King turns and looks into Olivia's eyes. "Go… go now!"

The raging fire in the Kingdom has spread to the spirit of Olivia. Her eyes are illuminated with determination. She swings the wooden door open and slams it behind her. Down the stone stairway she runs towards the front lines of battle. Her armor is shining from the torches set a blaze in the sconces as she storms forward. Her armor is superb, as if it has never seen battle, or perhaps she has never received a wound. Her armor is similar to the Triverian knights armor, bearing the star of Triveria on multiple plates of her armor, although hers is a shimmering silver lined with gold trim. Elegant, dignified, and sumptuous.

The King turns to the council members who are sitting around the stone map of Senary. "Who are these savages?"

"They appear to be citizens from the northern territory of Senary. They live off the land mostly."

"Why are they attacking my Kingdom! Our campaign has only been reaching south! They have no quarrel with us!" The King demands answers from the rest of the council. Though they remain silent. The King returns to the window, now seeing Amelia rushing towards Njal who has just killed the last knight within the platoon.

He yells out with a cry of war. He grips his wrist and shoves his arm upward. Relocating his shoulder back into place. Amelia is rushing headfirst towards him with her blade drawn. Her armor is already covered in a black powder from the ashes of the fire. Njal smiles wider.

"Are you a real warrior!?" He yells in his native language.

"I don't understand what you're saying! Speak my language!" Olivia thrusts her blade towards Njal.

"It appears not." Njal says arrogantly.

Njal brings his gigantic muscular arm downward onto the back of Amelia's neck. She drops to the ground and rolls over with her blade in the air. Blocking Njal's axe from ending her life. She sweeps around with her legs, knocking Njal over. She jumps to a stand and swings her sword downward towards his smiling face. With his free arm, he grips her hands. Stopping the strike instantly. With his axe, he drives it deep into her leg. Crippling her with one strike. She falls to her knee, screaming in pain.

"Bring me a real warrior!" Njal says in the Triverian tongue standing above Olivia.

"Who… are you?" Olivia looks upwards at Njal towering above her.

"I am Njal Thoreson!" Njal raises his axe into the sky as the King watches from the safety of his chamber above the Kingdom.

"Wait! Spare me! Please!" Olivia pleas to Njal.

With a thunderous roar, Njal brings his axe down into her skull. Piercing through her helmet as if it were made of paper. Olivia falls at his feet. An orange aura appears around her body and leaves as if her soul is running towards the afterlife.

"Is there no man, or woman who can give me what I desire!" Njal yells to the sky.

Upon looking up, he sees the King watching in shock from the clear window. His crown is sparkling in the reflection of the fire's glow. Njal points at the King. Sending a shock of fear deep into his bones. Njal steps over Olivia's body and walks towards the gates of the castle.

"Barricade the doors! That monster is coming!" The King yells to the council.

They quickly gather chairs and furniture and place them in front of the door. They all watch the door closely. They hear monstrous footsteps echoing up the stone stairway. With each step, their stomachs drop lower, and lower. As they approach the doorway. Njal speaks in his native tongue to them.

"What King hides while his kingdom is burnt to the ground!?" Njal kicks the door with enough force to crack the solid oak door instantly.

"Father!? What do we do!?" The Princess asks in fear.

"Pray..." The King says, swallowing his own tongue as fear shakes through his body.

Njal kicks the door again. Bending the iron hinges. And again, cracking the door a little more. He drives his blood-soaked axe through the door.

"Open this door!" Njal yells, kicking the door once again.

"Njal, patience." Leif says from behind him.

"Is there another!?" The King asks.

"Pardon our intrusion. King of Triveria. We promise safety to all who hide in this chamber if we may have a word." Leif says in the Triverian tongue.

"Who… who are you…?" The King asks cautiously.

"I am but a messenger from our leader. We demand conference. If you do not abide by our request, Njal will destroy this door and end your lives where you stand."

The King hesitates for what feels like an eternity, his body shaking in fear as he sees Njal looking through the large gash in the door. Piercing the King with his gaze like a blade through his heart. "Open…the door."

The council members unbarricade the door and open it slowly. Leif is standing in front of Njal, who is covered in blood and ash from the battle raging outside. Leif steps into the chamber with his hands behind his back, followed by Njal who must duck to enter the room. He glares at everyone inside, bringing the meaning of fear into reality.

"King of Triveria. Our leader wishes to send a message to you."

"What... is the message." The King says shaking in fear.

"That. Is our message." Leif points towards the window, where the Kingdom can be seen burning to ground and piling with bodies through the streets of blood.

The King is silent as the two men leave the room. Njal is dripping blood from his enormous body with each step.

"Wait! We will not allow you to leave!" One council member says with a frail aged voice.

Njal turns around and clamps his throat like a vice. The strength of his hand is like a bear. He squeezes with ferocity in his eyes, as a distinct snap shutters through the chamber. Njal drops the councilman's limp, lifeless body to the ground.

The Princess stares at the man in horror. In disbelief that he just snapped a man's neck with one hand. Shock and fear have overcome everyone in the room as they watch Njal stare at them in silence. Only the sound of his heavy breathing makes a sound.

"False. King." Njal utters in a grumbling low tone in the Triverian tongue, staring directly into the King's eyes.

Njal walks out of the room and down the stone stairs following Leif.

The King sits down on the chair that once barricaded the door, holding his chest as a panic attack has stricken his mind.

The King lowers his head into his hands. "My Queen is dead. My Kingdom is burning. My legacy is in ruin."

"Father... we can rebuild."

"I will make them regret ever coming to my Kingdom! I will have them all hung upon the walls of my castle! I will have my revenge!" The King yells as he is overcome with emotions void of happiness and joy.

"Father..." The Princess places her hand on the King's shoulders.

"Your highness. We must request that the legend take priority over anything. There will be no rebuilding if it were to come to fruition."

Tears fall down the King's face, he whips his head around towards the council. "To hell with the legend! I want retribution!"

The council watches as the King sobs in his chair. The Princess hugs him tight, crying tears of pain herself. The Kingdom burns to ashes as the

fires spread. The remaining Northmen cease their
attack and follow Njal and Leif as the knights all
stand in fear as they walk past. Afraid to make a
single move, worried that it will be their last. A
knight wearing red cords around his armor calls
orders to the knights near the castle, calling for
water and to stop the spread of the fire. The people
who remain in the Kingdom's walls run and cry in
the streets as the Northmen pass. Children without
mothers and fathers. Bodies piled in the rivers of
blood flowing downward as if the floodgates were
opened to a sea of wine. Black smoke rises from the
Kingdom in the late afternoon air as knights all
throughout the kingdom try to contain the fires.
Most diving into the flames to help those trapped,
and the others working together to snuff the flames.
The Kingdom of Triveria is in ruin, the spirits of all,
are deteriorated. The life they once knew, has been
brought to an immediate end. Though from the
ashes of atrocity, a determination for vengeance was
born. Every child who witnessed the attack, has a
hate growing within them. Every soldier that

survived, their tears of pain will turn into screams of anger. Everyone in the Kingdom, will forever yearn to bring death to those who slaughtered their loved ones.

"Sire." A green ring sitting upon the King's index finger glows and Captain Ankore's voice emanates from it.

"What is it… Captain?" The King says slowly sobbing.

"What is the status of the Kingdom? Is everyone alright?"

"The Kingdom is in ruin. Olivia is dead. The Kingdom is burning to the ground. My Queen… cannot be found. I fear she has died as well." The King says slowly as tears fall down his face.

"Sire… who did this?!" Ankore's yell almost shakes the room to the ground.

"The Northmen…" The King says softly.

Captain Ankore lowers his hand to his side, an uncontrollable anger begins to swell inside of him. Vengeance. His mind speaks to him softly. He turns and walks toward the fire where his platoon has gathered around, chatting amongst themselves. He returns to his seat next to Arthur and looks at him with sorrow in his eyes.

"What is the status of the Kingdom?" Arthur asks desperately.

"The Kingdom... is falling."

"Captain... what do you mean?"

"The King has told me that our Kingdom is burning, fires are raging through the streets. Olivia, the Tiger, has died in the battle. The King cannot find the Queen. I worry for the sake of our families." Ankore lowers his head and says solemnly.

Arthur lowers his head into his hands, crying and sobbing in the evening air. A cold wind blows through, but the anger the platoon feels is burning in their souls.

"Who are the attackers...?" Arthur asks from his lowered stance.

"The Northmen." Ankore looks towards Arthur.

"Why, why would they do this?"

"I do not know. But we will slaughter them all. Every single one." Ankore says with a vengeful, angry tone.

Arthur cries along with the other men in the platoon. Silently they sob with tears falling from each of their faces. Tears shed for their families, their homes, their kingdom.

"Men. Gather yourselves. Our Kingdom beckons for us to return. We move to Vorchid within the hour." Ankore stands and walks towards his horse.

The platoon stands, wiping their eyes and drying their noses. A smoldering determination and ferocity are born within each of their hearts.

Levi and Estelle make their way towards the estate of Isabella Ryker. Kristoff and Yovanna are sitting across the street inside of a restaurant as the sun falls over the Triverian mountains behind Vorchid. As they see Levi and Estelle, Kristoff places gold on the table and departs the store with Yovanna.

"There you two are! We have been waiting all day!" Kristoff yells from across the street.

"Sorry for making you wait. We stopped at a restaurant. It might be my last meal after all." Levi says, but Estelle nudges Levi on the arm looking at him with a glance of anger.

"Well, no time like the present. Let us go speak with Isabella. Oh, but knock first. There is…

just knock first." Kristoff says with embarrassment shaking his head

Levi looks towards the estate. "Something amiss?"

Kristoff walks towards the estate with the rest following him. "Well." Kristoff sighs. "Just knock first."

Kristoff gestures towards Levi to knock on the door. Levi lifts his shoulders and knocks willfully. Though, no answer, inside he hears two women being startled with the knock. Footsteps and rustling are heard from the outside of the home. Levi turns his head towards Kristoff, who just shakes his head. Suddenly the door opens. Isabella answers, her face is as red as it was when Kristoff and Yovanna first arrived.

"Oh! You are here. Good, come in. Maria is already here." She says with a smile holding the door.

The group walks in, Kristoff looks at her as he passes.

"I see you have found some clothes. Good for you." He says smugly.

Isabella smiles playfully with a fictitious innocence closing and locking the door behind them. She guides them to her study; the group enters and sees a map spread across the table. The map is detailed down to every store within Vorchid. Kristoff examines it closely with Levi, they are both looking at it with castigating stares.

"Maria, come to the study." Isabella says, peeking her head out of the door.

"Just a minute!" Maria yells from down the hall.

"Do you have measures in place for the city's defense?" Levi turns to Isabella.

"Yes, I have drawn out a route on the map. My guards will funnel the knights through the alleyways, giving my troops the advantage with ranged weapons." Maria follows the red line drawn on the map with her finger.

"That will not work." Kristoff says smugly.

"Of course, it will. This is not the first invasion my city has endured, and I'm sure it will not be the last." Isabella crosses her arms. The door creaks open, and Maria steps through. Panting and red in the face with a glass of water in her hand. Kristoff turns his head and looks at her for a moment.

"Engaging in a little bit of exercise, Maria?" Kristoff chuckles, causing Maria to become aggravated and embarrassed. Levi shakes his head and looks over Isabella's shoulder at the map.

"Kristoff is right. Ankore will not fall for that plan for a moment." Levi shakes his head.

"What do you two suggest I should do, since you know everything about defending a city?" Bella says arrogantly. Maria, Estelle, and Yovanna all stand in the background of the room, distancing themselves from each other without giving each other so much as a glance.

"How many guards do you have?" Levi asks Isabella, while studying the map.

"Three hundred or so." She answers.

"Not nearly as many as I had hoped. They will all die with this plan." Kristoff scoffs.

"The best chance for survival against the Triverian knights will be to fend them off outside of the city. Close quarters will be the downfall of this city." Levi says pointing to a field on the outskirts of Vorchid.

"I agree. Forming two walls of one hundred men each will be the most advantageous. They will expect that the best warriors will be on the front lines and likely match the power. Our best bet will be to try and outnumber them, your guards will certainly not outmatch them." Kristoff draws lines on the map where the guards will have their best chance of survival.

Levi crosses his arms and looks towards Isabella. "We will need to barricade the entrances to the city once the guards are outside. Have the remainder of your guards hold the main entrance, it is the best chance if they were to slaughter the first two hundred. Though if they were to break through the barricaded entrance and slaughter the remaining troops, this city will fall before morning."

"That is absurd. There are fifty of them against three hundred of us. My guards will wipe them out before they even step foot in this city." Isabella wraps her hips with her hands and scowls at Levi.

"No, they are right, Bella. Ankore's men are the fiercest warriors of the Kingdom. These men are the same who led the conquest for the King. They have taken over nearly half of this continent on their own. They are merciless, ruthless murderers." Maria says with a sincere tone.

"Fine... I will block the entrances to the city, and have the guards prepare for battle. If these knights are truly this gruesome of warriors, then I demand you two join the battle if the walls of my city fall. I will not have my brother's death be in vain."

"If it comes down to it. I will give myself up. There is no need for an entire city to be destroyed for my sake." Levi says solemnly.

Estelle looks to Levi with puffed cheeks and a frown sprawled on her face. "Levi... no."

"Come on, let us prepare ourselves." Levi says to the group. Levi walks out of Isabella's study with his four companions.

Isabella peers over her map placing her hands on the desk. She looks at the map as tears fall from her face.

"I cannot let my city fall... Johnathan, you're gone. You are all that I had left... And they have taken you from me... First father... now you... I do not wish to be alone in this world, Vorchid is the legacy our father built. I will not let it fall!" She slams her balled fists on the desk as tears stream down her face, dripping on the map.

As the sun finally creeps over the mountains behind Vorchid. The moon shines through the trees illuminating the path towards Vorchid, glistening on the billowing snowdrift. Ankore and his men saddle their horses in the forest just across the open fields of Vorchid's farmlands. Ankore watches as an army lines the main entrance of the city. He looks to the two fourth Edict members to his right and left. Arthur is sitting atop his large black horse on the right of Ankore, while Mattaeus is mounted on a brown and white horse to his left.

"Sir, it seems they have been informed of our presence." Mattaeus watches the guards fall into a formation, readying their blades and shields.

"So, it would seem..." Ankore says as his face turns to a scowl.

Ankore places his helm over his head. He pulls the reins of his horse, turning towards his men.

"For the Kingdom!" He yells to his men, drawing his sword to the sky.

"For Triveria!" His men synchronously yell back.

The platoon of knights charges forward towards the wall of guards protecting the gates of Vorchid. Their steeds thunderously roar through the night air. Ankore and the remaining members of the fourth Edict ride behind them. An aura of ferocity and death fill the air. People within Vorchid watch from the streets and their homes as their guards' line up to defend the city. The citizens hide their sons and daughters in fear of their protection. The merchants gather their things and recede back into their stores, locking the doors and placing cloths over the windows. Lok is sharpening a beautifully crafted short sword with an angle forty-five degrees. He looks outside, seeing the busy streets clear out quickly. People are running into their homes and barricading their doors as if the end of times has come for them.

"So, it is upon us." Lok says with a sorrow filled smile. "May the Gods be with you both." He says picturing Estelle and Levi in his shop once more.

Levi and Kristoff are standing at the rear of the guards within the barricaded walls of the city. Kristoff looks to Levi with concern in his eyes. He lifts his helmet over his head and slides it on, strapping it under his chin tightly. Maria watches with Isabella from a balcony overlooking the streets. Isabella's heart is racing, fearing the destruction and death the knights in black armor are coming to unleash upon her home. Estelle wraps Levi's cloak around her shoulders. She opens the door from Maria's home, looking to the fields over the river flowing through the Vorchid canal. She sees the black armor of the knights and her heart begins to race. She is overcome with fear for Levi's well-being. A snowfall begins over the fields and streets, dropping visibility to near zero. The snow came from nowhere, it is as if the God's have rolled the dice in favor of the Triverian platoon.

"We have the advantage!" Arthur yells to the platoon. "We were born in the frost, and they will die by it!" He yells charging forward to the front of the platoon.

His thunderous stomps shake the souls of the guards, though ready for battle, none are ready for slaughter.

Estelle runs to Levi through the thick blizzard that has hidden the battle from the eyes of the townspeople. She stands next to Levi with her hand on her bow. Ready to fight whenever she can.

Levi looks down towards her. "Estelle."

"Do not tell me to run. I will stand by you until the end." She says without looking up at him.

Kristoff chuckles. "She is a good one for you. Bull headed and altruistic to the core."

"Do not do anything rash. If they break through the lines. I want you to stay back. Maria has a plan if they do." He says.

Estelle nods and looks through the thick wall of snow.

"I can't see anything." She says.

"This snow will be the downfall of the guards. They are not used to battle in these conditions. Triverians are." Kristoff shakes his head in disbelief over the blizzard that appeared out of nowhere.

Suddenly the sounds of battle ring through the wall of snow. The distinct sound of metal clashing with metal, followed by the sound of a blade piercing flesh. The screams begin, both the screams of war, and the screams of pain. A silence has overcome the streets, the guards standing behind the barricades watch intently. Though the snow has blocked their view. Silently Levi, Kristoff, and Estelle listen. Levi's mind is being enveloped with a sea of wrath as his eyes flash before him. The sight of his mother's death appears again and again.

Arthur and Mattaeus have advanced to the front of the platoon. Arthur is quickly dispersing the guards as if they were no more than practice dummies in his path. Mattaeus has locked blades with three guards, though seems to be holding his own. Ankore watches from the back of the platoon as his knights devour the lives of the guards. For every knight that falls, ten guards are falling at their feet. The guards are being pushed back towards the freezing cold canal behind them. The knights press forward in groups of five, holding off and slaughtering groups of ten or more guards at one. Blood has drenched the snow; a path of scarlet has illuminated the once strong line of guards.

"Push! Push them into the canal!" Ankore yells out from the rear.

"Push!" The knights that are locked in a game of blades yell out. Driving their feet into the snow.

The knight's brute strength easily overpowers the guards who are untrained and unconditioned. The rear line of guards meets the stone foundation of the canal. Many of them lose their focus and look backwards into the icy water that is crying out to them. With another forceful push, the rear line of guards falls back into the icy depths. They all try to swim upwards, but their heavy armor matches with the shock of the freezing water they sink to their icy depths with more guards piling on top of their bodies. A group of guards push through their attacking knights due to the knight's overconfidence. They rush towards Ankore with their blades drawn and bloody.

"Captain!" Arthur yells from the front, pulling his blade from the throat of a guard.

Captain Ankore finally draws his blade and calmly walks towards the group of ten guards rushing towards him. A green aura glows around him. With a quick strike he decapitates one of the guards. Two swing their blades towards his chest. With a quick maneuver, he turns his body and avoids the strike. He kicks one in the chest, knocking both over and denting the plate armor. Another guard yells and thrusts his blade towards Ankore. Ankore grabs the man's arm with his free hand and guides his thrust into the throat of one of the men on the ground. He slices through their thin chainmail around the necks of the other two. They fall to the ground bleeding profusely as the moan in pain and cough up blood.

The Captain looks to the remaining men standing before him in shock over the prowess in battle. In fear of the monster of a man standing before them. Ankore yells with a powerful battle cry, rushing towards the men with ferocity in his eyes. His magical aura glows stronger with each life he takes, though it is the same unstable green aura that appeared in his temporary home in Drixyl. Screaming Levi's name.

Arthur watches his Captain slaughter the men who attacked him, alone. As if they were nothing but sword practice. Watching the endeavor fuels Arthur's fighting spirit. With a powerful yell, he rushes forward to the barricade blocking their entrance to the city. He bulls through the first as if it were nothing more than paper. The barrels and chests stacked to create a wall crash to the ground. He continues like a raging bull towards the one hundred man standing behind the second barricade.

"Prepare yourselves!" One guard calls out to his brothers and sisters.

"Lord, what an obnoxious animal." Kristoff says watching Arthur bust through the second barricade as if he were a stampeding wild animal. "Levi, we may have to step in. Arthur is a monster in the body of a man."

"Maria! Now!" Levi calls out to Maria standing on the balcony.

Estelle and Kristoff turn around and watch Maria. Isabella steps away, Maria raises her arms to the sky. A lilac colored aura appears around her. She lets out a deep breath as the aura moves to her hands. She opens her eyes; a purple glow appears from them as she juts her hands forwards. A wall of flames appears on each side of the street. Ankore looks to the city, seeing the distinct high-level magic being used. He shakes his head and walks forward through the deep snow. Feeling the pressure of Maria's magic aura radiate into his body. He steps over bodies of the guards bleeding profusely in the deep snow, slicing through any who dare try to strike him down in his path. The platoon of knight's force through the last standing wall of guards outside of the city and advance inward behind Arthur, who is draining the life from the forces of the last wall of defense single handedly.

Levi draws his blade and moves Estelle behind him. He looks towards Kristoff who matches his glare. They nod at each other and step towards what would seem like certain death to any man who dares to match blades with the knights. Estelle tries to follow behind them but is stopped by Maria who grabs her shoulder and shakes her head at Estelle. She breaks free and runs to Levi and Kristoff but is pushed backwards by a wall of magical flames that appear just in front of her.

"Maria! Let me go!" She yells back to Maria, who shakes her head once more.

Estelle looks through the purple and blue flames, she sees Levi and Kristoff match blades with a group of knights as the remaining guards begin to fall. Suddenly the wall of flames opened as if someone tore through them with holy water. Yovanna lowers her hands and breathes out steadily. She walks towards Estelle, glaring at Maria intently as she walks past.

"I will not allow this!" Maria yells to the two.

"If you are too afraid to fight. Then go hide away!" Estelle angrily retorts, walking through the wall of flames with Yovanna.

Maria shakes her head and looks through the tear, seeing Levi and Kristoff slicing through the Triverian Knights steadily Arthur and Mattaeus fight their way towards them. She swallows her tongue and walks through the flames, closing the tear behind her. The smell of death and burning flesh defecate in her nostrils.

Estelle draws her bow and loosens multiple arrows quickly towards the knights, taking the lives of one for every arrow.

"Estelle! I told you to stay back!" Levi says with disdain in his voice.

"I will not leave you to fight alone!" Estelle yells, drawing her bow back once again.

Levi shakes his head and clashes swords with another knight. Levi kicks the knight in the abdomen and pierces through his chest with the tip of his blade.

"This is fun, is it not? Just like old times." Kristoff says cheerfully to Levi.

"Fun is not the word I would use." Levi says striking the side of another knight with his sword.

A powerful yell and thunderous stomping shake their bodies. Arthur rushes towards them like a raging bull. Arthur picks up Levi and throws him backwards, knocking his breath away from his body.

"That hurt." Levi says rolling over and standing up.

Kristoff tries to strike Arthur from the rear, but Mattaeus stops his blade with his own.

"Traitor!" He yells at Kristoff, in a fierce standoff with his former squad leader.

"Oh, shut up, you little runt." Kristoff scoffs, breaking away from the clasp and knocking him over.

Arthur raises his sword and strikes downward with the force of a bear. Levi blocks the strike, though almost loses his footing in the blood running down the stone road from the numerous slain corpses in the battle's wake.

"You are the reason my family is not safe! I should be there! Protecting them! Not hunting a murderer like you!" Arthur strikes Levi's blade again and again.

Levi blocks his attacks with elegant skill. "You chose this fate!"

Levi ducks through the opening in Arthur's wide stance. Before he can get a chance to strike him down. Arthur's massive arm swings around, knocking Levi over like a ragdoll. His helmet falls from his head and rolls across the stone path.

"Levi!" Estelle yells, loosening another arrow for Arthur.

The arrow lands in between the plates of his chest armor. Piercing him in the back.

"You little witch!" Arthur yells, picking up a sword from the street and aiming to throw it at Estelle.

Levi quickly jumps to his feet and thrusts his sword through Arthur's massive chest. Arthur falls to his knees, holding the sword that is pierced through his body.

"My family..." Arthur coughs up blood, with tears streaming down from under his helmet. "I will be with you soon, my dear." He says falling forward in the blood-soaked street. Levi pulls his blade from the giant's chest and looks to Estelle who smiles at him with the same smile that warmed his heart the day they met.

"Levi! Quit making lovey eyes at Estelle and help me! I am a bit rusty it seems!" Kristoff yells out to his friend.

Levi turns and sees Kristoff on his back with Mattaeus sitting atop of him. Mattaeus' blade is nearly piercing Kristoff's throat. Before Levi can even take a step to help his friend, a flame bursts from the wall towards Mattaeus. Knocking him off Kristoff instantly. Kristoff turns his head while breathing heavy and looks towards Yovanna who had just saved his life. Kristoff leaps to his feet in an instant and pounces on Mattaeus, wrapping his hands around his throat tightly.

"Just so you know. This is personal. I have never liked you." Kristoff spits in Mattaeus face, while choking the life from him.

Kristoff stands from the lifeless body of his old comrade. Panting, fatigued, and covered in blood from the knights slain by his blade. He looks at Levi, who is watching him intently from a few feet away. Yovanna, Estelle, and Maria join their little grouping and look at each other in silence.

"There is no time to chat really, we still have a ways to go before we can take a breather." Kristoff continues. "Thank you, as well, Yovanna." He says with an innocent smile.

Yovanna smiles back while Estelle and Maria shake their heads. Their moment of peace is disrupted as quickly as it began.

"Levi!" Ankore yells from the distance. "Come and face me brother!"

Levi looks around to his group of companions as guards struggle to finish off the remaining handful of knights.

"Stay here. All of you. This is my fight." Levi says walking forward.

"No!" Estelle grabs his arm. "I'm coming too. Your fight is my fight."

"Estelle. I refuse."

Kristoff holds his open hand out to Levi. "Levi, we'll face him as real brothers. We will end this madness."

Levi grabs his hand and holds it tightly. He looks around to Maria, then Yovanna, and finally Estelle. He smiles and nods. He walks forward through the streets, stepping over the corpses glistening in the magical walls of flame surrounding the street. Everyone walking next to him as they approach the terrifying yells of Captain Ankore. Levi is the first to cross the bridge, his eyes are tortured with the sight of slaughter. Every guard that was sent to their death by his plan weighs heavy on his mind, he looks around with each step. He looks at Captain Ankore who is standing in the distance with an ominous green aura emanating from his body. Levi's anger is reaching his breaking point, seeing his brother once again, alone. The same person, who took their mother's life with his own hands.

"Finally, I will have my vengeance!" Ankore yells rushing towards Levi with his blade drawn.

The green aura emanating from Ankore's body is exerting a pressure as if they each ran into a brick wall without moving one step. Levi meets Ankore's blade with his, rushing forward and pushing Ankore away from the group. Kristoff draws his blade and Estelle readies her bow.

"This is my fight! Stay out of it!" Levi yells, throwing Ankore backwards into the snow.

The two clash blades repeatedly, Levi's aura becomes black and begins exerting a stronger pressure than Ankore's. Fiercely the two fight in the snow. The sound of their battle cries and the chime of their swords ring through everyone's ears as they watch the fatal battle between the two brothers.

"I cannot stand here and watch this!" Estelle says, drawing a dagger from a sheath at her hip and rushing towards Ankore and Levi.

"Estelle. Stop!" Kristoff reaches for her arm but misses. Maria, Kristoff, and Yovanna rush after her.

Ankore notices Estelle rushing at him with a dagger, he kicks Levi to the side and lunges towards her with the tip of his sword.

Levi's mind draws the world to almost a complete stop as he falls backwards, watching Captain Ankore lunge at Estelle. The ferocity in Estelle's eyes that are glistening in the moonlight meet Levi's as she looks towards him. Ankore's blade just a few inches from her chest. She mouths something to Levi, though he cannot make it out. His head falls backwards, smashing on a helmet of one of the fallen knights. His mind begins to fade to black as he hears the scream of a woman, and the distinct sound of a blade piercing flesh He looks upwards as he begins to lose consciousness, he sees Ankore's blade pierce through Estelle's body. The twinkle in her eyes becomes dim as the shock of the blade piercing through her body sends her into shock.

"Estelle!" He hears Maria call out as his mind fades to black.

Kristoff strikes Ankore across the chest, though his strike does not cut through his thick plate armor.

"You have taken everything from me Levi! Now it's my turn to take everything from you!" He yells to Levi as he watches from the ground, seeing Ankore pull his sword from Estelle's body.

Estelle falls backwards, Maria stops her fall and catches her. Estelle begins to cough up blood as her life fades from her body. Maria looks to Levi, who's black aura has now grown immensely and has begun to melt the snow and disintegrate the ground around him as he tries to stand.

"We have to go! Now!" Maria yells to Kristoff who is locked into a clash with Ankore.

"I'm not leaving Levi here alone!" He yells out, pushing Ankore backwards into the snow.

"Now!" Maria yells.

"Levi!" Kristoff yells out reaching towards him.

Before he can reach Levi's unconscious body, the black aura pushes him backwards into Yovanna. Maria grabs Yovanna's arm and in a flash of purple, they disappear into the night air.

"The King warned me of this. He told me you were the embodiment of a demon. I did not want to believe him. But now I see the truth." Ankore looks to Levi's body as it is exerting an immense magical aura.

Ankore walks toward Levi, pushing through the black aura surrounding him. Ankore drives his blade deep into Levi's leg.

"I will make you suffer. Just as you have made me suffer, brother." Ankore pulls his blade from Levi's leg.

Levi's comrades appear in a forest above Vorchid, on top of the plateau where Levi had teleported himself and Estelle away from Drixyl. Kristoff and Yovanna crawl to Estelle's side as Maria lays her next to the body of the Wyvern Levi had slain just days ago. They all watch as Maria desperately tries to heal Estelle. She begins to cough up more blood.

"Levi... where's Levi?" Estelle struggles to say, looking towards Maria as her vision fades to black.

Chapter 10: Awaken the Wolf

Levi has entered the realm of the void once again. The torches are surrounding him, though his body is engulfing the void around him entirely. He is on his knees with tears falling from his face as the tornado like void is swirling into him. He feels a hand on his shoulder, he turns his crying eyes around, though no one is there.

"My son. Do not cry." The voice of Levi's birth mother says into his ear softly.

"I cannot stop. I have lost everything… My home, my father, my mother, the woman I've feelings for, my life. It is gone. It is all…gone." Tears of blood fall down his face like a river as he overflows with a swelling anger inside of him.

"You have not lost. It is time to let go, it is time to release the rage you have held deep within you for so long. It is no longer possible to contain within your mind."

"How!? How can I let go!? She is gone! I have failed her! I've failed everyone!" Levi cries out in anger.

"Atone. My son. Atone for your sins." Levi's mother says as her voice dissipates from his ears.

"Son. It is not about how, or why. To answer your questions, ask yourself who. For whom, do you live for?" Levi's father appears in front of him as if he were standing there the entire time.

The tears of blood pool around Levi as he kneels in the swirling void. "Father, what do you mean? Who do I live for?"

"Ask yourself that question. It is your only way to atone for your sins. You have held back every ounce of anger you have felt your entire life. You have plagued your mind and soul with thoughts of destruction and terror, while you have lived a life full of kindness and peace. Right now, your brother is trying to end your life. Your magic is healing you faster than he can harm you, though it will not last forever. You must choose, son. Choose wisely. Whom, do you live for?"

"I do not understand! You are asking why I live!"

"Exactly. Who made you refrain from giving yourself over to your brother and being taken to the kingdom? Who kept your mind from eating your soul? Who have you kept living for?" His father asks, kneeling in front of him and placing his hand on his shoulder.

Levi looks up from the black void swirling around him and into his father's eyes.

"Estelle..." Levi says as the tears of blood fall down his face like a river.

Levi's father chuckles as he fades from the swirling void. "Exactly. Didn't think I would have to force it out of you."

"Father!? Do not go!" Levi yells.

"Levi, are you going to keep this within your mind as well? Your brother ended my life, and as your eyes have shown you. He took the life of Amelia, and now he has taken the life of Estelle. What is next, will he take the lives of your friends as well? He is attempting to take your life at this moment. What will you do?" Levi's adoptive mother asks, placing her chin on the top of his head.

Levi looks into the swirling void as his adoptive mother disappears in front of his eyes. A burning wrath has taken over his mind, body, and soul. His eyes are no longer blue, but instead as black as night. The swirling void comes to a stop as the torches illuminate the empty room within Levi's mind. It is no longer surrounded in a void. It has become a blank slate of Levi's mind as each torch starts to flicker with a black glow as if the demons have broken through the gates of hell into Levi's mind.

"What will you do?" The three voices within Levi's head speak to him softly in his ear as the torches flicker violently.

Levi comes to a stand as the tears of blood slowly stop, the black aura flows from his body, uncontrollable, unstable, destructive, and the demonic essence of chaos. "I... will... atone."

Levi opens his eyes as Ankore's blade comes down towards his head like a bolt of lightning striking water. Levi stops the blade with his bare hands and stands as if he were not even injured from the numerous strikes from Ankore's blade.

"How!? How are you alive, you demon!?" Ankore yells in fear as he looks into the now black eyes of Levi.

"I... will... atone...." Levi says in a soft voice to his brother.

Suddenly the entire area is filled with a black aura. The aura engulfs a large radius around Levi, along with the slain bodies in the field and canal. The magical flames blazing in the streets are put out instantly as Levi's aura envelops them with its darkness. The townspeople in their homes look towards the field where Levi and Ankore were fighting. But, it is as if the moon's light no longer shines upon Senary.

"I will atone!" Levi yells, gripping Ankore's blade and disintegrating it in the aura.

"Demon! You are the Devil!" Ankore yells.

The area Levi's aura has engulfed is disintegrated instantly in an immense explosion of magic. Levi's aura explodes into the sky with black streaks of lightning swirling around the area. Kristoff looks over the plateau, watching the area where the battle is taking place. A shockwave shakes the ground beneath his feet, followed by the sound of what seems to be an earthquake. Kristoff covers his eyes with his arm.

"Get down!" He yells to the women behind him on the plateau.

The explosion of magic disappears in the blink of an eye, with only what appears to be black wings of a demon above the epicenter, that soon dissipate into the winter air. Everything within the radius of Levi has disintegrated into nothing nearly twelve feet deep from where Levi was standing. The buildings engulfed in the explosion vanished as if they were never there. The canal is destroyed causing water to crash into the massive crater. The slain bodies disappear along with the streets and fields of Vorchid. Isabella looks over the balcony in shock, covering her mouth as tears fall down her face, realizing Vorchid is nearly destroyed.

"Levi!" Kristoff yells from over the plateau.

Levi is standing in the center of the explosion, his armor torn to shreds as he stares at the ashes of his brother fluttering away in the wind. Levi's mind falls blank and he drops to his knees letting out a deep breath. He falls forward in the massive crater with blue lightning zapping the ground near him. Levi's body dissipates just as the wings above him did. His body becomes a husk as his armor rolls over the ash that has become his remains. As his body crumbles, a black figure appears over his armor. That of a wolf.

"Finally." The Wolf whispers as it looks towards the sky.

The clouds transmute from a luscious white to a vivid black, and swirl like a hurricane at the epicenter of the battlefield. The Wolf bares its teeth towards the sky, but with a smile.

"I have waited...for too long." The Wolf whispers towards the sky as it fades into the air.

The clouds return to normal, yet the stench of malice fills the world like an early morning fog.

"Kristoff come here! Estelle is in bad shape!" Maria calls out.

Kristoff rushes to her side, as Estelle coughs up blood and gasps for air.

"I think the blade pierced her lungs. I do not know if my magic can heal this severe of a wound."

"What do you need me to do!?" Kristoff holds pressure on Estelle's wound.

"I… can give her my life. It is the only way to save her." Yovanna says softly as she approaches the trio.

Maria looks to Yovanna as blood from Estelle's quickly fading body covers her hands. "What do you mean? You can just give her your life?"

"She is only in this because of me. I will do it." Yovanna says moving Maria out of the way.

Yovanna places her hands overtop of Estelle's wound and takes a deep breath as her body glows with a swirling aura of white and green.

"Divine ones. Take my soul and heal thy wounds. Give life to which is fallen. One. For. One." Yovanna chants slowly with increasingly sporadic breathing.

In the blink of an eye, Yovanna's aura protrudes into the sky and opens a window through the clouds. The revealing light shines on Estelle's body. Her wound closes and her body trembles from the aura that has now engulfed her unconscious body.

Yovanna falls to the ground as the clouds close once again, darkening the sky. Maria and Kristoff watch as the entire process is over in a flash. They look towards each other in shock, and down at Estelle. She opens her beautiful amethyst eyes once again.

Estelle jolts up. "Where is Levi?!" She yells out.

"I believe he is still down there with Ankore, but there was a bit of excitement just a few moments ago." Kristoff says with hesitation.

"Where are we?" She asks.

"We are on the plateau where the Wyvern was killed. Maria got us to safety in the nick of time it seems. Estelle, are you feeling alright?" Kristoff asks, examining Estelle.

"I'm a little drowsy, but I feel fine. Why?"

Maria turns her head to the lifeless body of Yovanna lying on the ground. "She gave her life to heal you, Estelle."

"She what? Why would she do that?"

"Perhaps she wished to atone. We will give her a proper burial. We need to find Levi immediately. I can take us back to where we were. Give me your hands, Kristoff, take hold of Yovanna."

Kristoff nods his head and lifts Yovanna into his arms. Estelle grabs Maria's arm and Maria holds Kristoff's shoulder. In a flash, they return to the epicenter of the explosion, examining the chaos that has ensued from the short clash of blades between two former brothers.

"What in the hell happened here?" Kristoff asks, looking around the destroyed battlefield.

Maria lowers her head. "This was the power Levi kept away. This was the destruction within his mind that I saw."

"No, this cannot be. This is wrong!" Estelle yells, running towards Levi's armor that is lying on the ground.

"Levi!" She yells out.

She falls to her knees directly next to Levi's battered and torn armor and begins to cry. "Levi! Levi! No!" She cries, lifting his helmet to her head as what appears to be ash sprinkles out.

Maria walks to her side as she begins to cry as well. Maria kneels next to Estelle as tears fall into the ashen lain ground. "He lost control. I was afraid of this."

"What do you mean!? Why did you not help him!?"

"I could not. Only the Amaranthine could. And you have failed." Maria says in tears, lifting Levi's pendant his father had given him long ago, that is glowing with a blue aura. "Take this. Let this be a memory of your failures." Maria says, handing Estelle the sword.

Estelle's cries become harder and she begins to choke and cough.

Kristoff is in shock over the husk that was once his best friend. Tears slowly fall as he lowers his head. "I'll see you again, brother." He says softly.

"Come on, we must attend to the damage." Maria says walking towards the remains of Vorchid.

Estelle remains kneeling and crying, holding Levi's pendant and his helm.

Within the chamber of the legend, the council gather around the flickering blue flames. They watch the legend intently as lights swirl throughout the room. It is as if the souls of the fallen marked ones have come to their resting place, but only for a moment before disappearing into the blue fire in the center of the room. The legend begins to glow red, shadowing the entire room in a bright light.

The council members watch intently as the marks begin to glow. The Mark of the Ox, now illuminated red, followed by the Mark of the Tiger, and finally the Mark of the Boar. The red glow becomes dim as the radiant blue flames reassume their position in the room, now glowing steadily.

"It appears that Ankore has failed, and in return, lost his life to the demon."

"Yes, it appears that way. Now all that remains is the Serpent, the Raven, and the Wolf."

"What shall we do?"

"We have no choice; we no longer have the means of having the demon and the Amaranthine delivered to us. We must lure him here. Perhaps the destruction of the Kingdom will work in our favor."

"Yes. I agree. The hungry Wolf will come for its prey."

"Yes, the demon will rise through the flames of the Kingdom to devour the life of the one who took from him."

"The King must lure the Wolf, the King will feed the demon, the King must atone."

"The King must atone for his sins." The council says synchronously in the glow of the steady blue flames.

The King paces back and forth in his throne room. His daughter, she who bears the Mark of the Serpent watches intently as he angrily paces. A knock echoes through the throne room, followed by the creaking of the great iron door as it swings open. Through the door enters the entire council, their hoods back and their heads held low. Each one with silver hair, and aged skin.

"What brings you to my throne room?" The King stops and turns to the council.

"The demon has devoured the souls of two of the marked. First your child, followed by his own brother." One council member raises her head and says.

The King's frustration grows within him. His mind is filled with sorrow, and rage. Tears stream down his face as he falls to his knees in the spacious throne room.

"What must I do...?" The King says softly to the council.

"You must lure the demon into the walls of your Kingdom."

"How... how can I draw him here?" The King asks desperately.

"Offer yourself as sacrifice to the demon. Offer your soul to the wolf. He will come, he will come to devour your soul. Only then will we be able to stop the prophecy."

The King looks to the ceiling. "I... understand..."

Upon the ceiling is a portrait of the past leaders of the Kingdom of Triveria. His father, and his father before him, and his father before that.

"Three hundred years, my Kingdom has reigned as the most powerful in Senary. If I must give my soul to the devil to allow my Kingdom to prosper for a thousand more. I will do just that." The King says standing to his feet and yelling out to Levi. "Do you hear me demon!? I offer my soul to you! I will allow you to devour the essence of my life! Come to me! Feast on my soul!" The King yells.

"Father…" The princess watches in horror as the King's mind begins to slip.

Across Senary, the villages surrounding the ancient structures belonging to the Sacred Six of Legend begin to glow with the respective aura of their fallen vessels. The ominous black fog flows from the edges as the lights fueled by magic of the soul shoot into the sky. The fog swallows every area surrounding the ancient structures, deteriorating and destroying everything it touches. Villagers begin to fall to their knees coughing violently, suffocating from the fog. People all around Senary look in the direction of the ancient structures. Watching as the lights appear in the sky. Silently they watch, some panic, others fall to their knees and pray to their God to forgive their sins, believing the end of times is upon them.

On a small boat floating blissfully down the icy rivers of Senary. The Queen of Triveria and another woman watch as the lights appear all around Senary.

"My Queen... what are these lights?" The woman asks.

"My father told me of them once. They are the souls of the fallen Sacred Six. We must find Levi as soon as we can. We must put an end to this madness!" The Queen says watching the lights shoot through the sky in the rising sun.

Estelle is sitting alone in her cabin just outside of the ransacked town of Drixyl. Three days past the battle. The moonlight peeks through the window, and her eyes are flickering in the glow of the fire keeping her home warm. A stacked suit of shredded armor is sitting next to her as she sits on the ground sobbing and crying in the night, along with a sheathed sword leaning against it. Estelle is sobbing and crying as she holds Levi's pendant tight close against her chin.

The pendant glows dimly with a deep blue aura on the howling wolf. Through her tear-filled eyes, she sees the faint glow.

A voice speaks out to her. "Estelle."

To be continued.

Made in the USA
Middletown, DE
07 January 2022

58063839R00262